BROKEN HEARTS

BROKEN REBEL BROTHERHOOD: NEXT GENERATION

ANDI RHODES

For Darcie - Without your unwavering support and help, Tillie and Isaiah's story may never have been told. You have become one of my best friends and I'm forever grateful that you are a part of my journey and my life!

ALSO BY ANDI RHODES

Broken Rebel Brotherhood

Broken Souls

Broken Innocence

Broken Boundaries

Broken Rebel Brotherhood: Complete Series Box set

Broken Rebel Brotherhood: Next Generation

Broken Hearts

Broken Wings

Broken Mind

Bastards and Badges

Stark Revenge

Slade's Fall

Jett's Guard

Soulless Kings MC

Fender

Joker

Piston

Greaser

Riker

Trainwreck

Squirrel

Gibson

Satan's Legacy MC

Snow's Angel

Toga's Demons

Magic's Torment

BROKEN REBEL BROTHERHOOD

THE ORIGINALS

When two people are destined for each other, a place can never be too far, waiting can never be too long, and even the strongest force can't ever tear them apart.

-Unknown

PROLOGUE

TILLIE

"What the fuck do you want from me?"

"I want you to stay!" I shout.

Isaiah stands in front of me with his arms crossed over his lean chest and a glare that would scare most people. But I'm not most people. I've grown up with Isaiah and know him better than even he knows himself.

"You know I can't do that," he says. He drops his arms to his sides and closes the distance between us. "Babe, you knew I was leaving today."

My eyes burn with unshed tears. I refuse to let him see the sadness. I'm much more comfortable with anger. I give a sharp nod, not trusting my voice.

"What kind of Brother will I make if I don't go?" He cups my cheek. "Besides, it's only boot camp. I'll be at the Navy Recruit Training Command in Illinois. It's not like it's far."

"Far enough," I mumble under my breath.

Isaiah chuckles and leans in to press his lips against mine. "It'll be over before you know it."

"Eight weeks," I shriek. "Eight weeks with no phone calls, no texts, nothing."

"But then you'll see me at graduation," he soothes. "Tillie, please don't make this harder than it is."

I pull away from him and start to pace. He's right. I'm making this hard. I know it's not easy for him to leave the only home he's ever known, his family, *me*. We've been inseparable for as long as I can remember, and the thought of not even being able to talk to him sends me into panic mode.

"I'm sorry," I say when I stop pacing. "It's just—"

"You ready, son?"

Uncle Micah—who's not really my uncle—steps up behind Isaiah and puts his hands on his shoulders. Aunt Sadie is right next to him, silent tears running down her cheeks.

"In a minute, Pops," Isaiah says gruffly.

"Okay. But only a minute. You don't want to be late."

"Late?" Isaiah laughs. "Not likely if you're driving."

"Better check that before you leave," Uncle Micah says. "You won't be able to unleash the smart ass at boot camp."

"Give him a break," Aunt Sadie cuts in. "Let's give them another minute."

They walk away, leaving me alone with the love of my life. I step closer to him and wrap my arms around his waist and rest my cheek on his chest. His heartbeat thumps wildly, and I savor the sound and feel of it.

"You're gonna be okay, babe," Isaiah says into my hair. "You're stronger than you think."

"I don't feel very strong right now."

"I know. But when the eight weeks are up, I'll find out where I'll be stationed, and we can plan from there. You can move to be closer or I'll visit often. We'll make it work. I promise."

"Yeah, yeah okay."

"C'mon," he says and takes a step back to look me in the eyes. "Give me a kiss to hold me over."

I press my lips to his, and within seconds, we're lost in a kiss that temporarily distracts me from what's happening. My hair is wrapped around Isaiah's fingers, and his tongue eases it's way past my lips and into the recesses of my mouth.

A moan escapes me, and I jump up to lock my ankles at the small of his back. Locked against his body, I forget that we're surrounded by our families and other members of the Broken Rebel Brotherhood. I forget everything else but how it feels to be with him, against him.

"That's enough," my dad barks from behind us.

Isaiah ends the kiss, and I slide down his body to let my feet hit the ground. I look over my shoulder at my dad and glare. He's the only person who doesn't seem to care that I'm hurting right now.

"It's time, babe," Isaiah whispers.

I nod and swipe at the tears that I can no longer stop from falling. "I love you."

"I love you too." Isaiah gives me one last quick peck on the lips. "I'll see you soon."

With that, he turns away and struts toward his dad. Isabelle, Isaiah's twin and one of my best friends, gets in the backseat with him, and their parents get in the front. Within minutes, dust billows and the Jeep disappears from view.

A soft hand grazes mine and I glance down to see Lila, my younger sister, standing next to me.

"I'm gonna miss him too," she says with a small smile.

"We all will," my mom says from next to Lila.

"This'll be good for him," my dad says from my other side. He wraps his arm around my shoulders and pulls me toward him. "And it'll be good for you too. Give you both a chance to figure out what you want outta life."

I yank out of his hold and stare him down. I've perfected the look over the years, but it doesn't faze him. I don't think it ever did.

"Really, Aiden?" my mom remarks.

"What?" Dad throws his arms in the air. "Jesus, Scarlett. You know as well as I do that they need some space. They both need to see what's out there in the world."

"Cause that worked out so well for Mom," I say with venom.

"Tillie!" Dad shouts and I instantly regret the words. My mom's dark past is a sore subject in my family. "Apologize to your mother. Now."

I turn toward my mom and give an apologetic smile. "I'm sorry."

"I know, baby." She tips my chin up. "I know you're hurting and I'm sorry for that. But it will be okay. You're my daughter, after all."

"Peanut, come with me," my dad instructs and walks toward the house without waiting to see if I follow.

I glance at my mom who simply shrugs her shoulders and tips her head to indicate that I should do as I'm told. With a giant sigh, I trudge across the driveway, up the steps, and into the living room where my dad is waiting on me.

"Sit down," he demands and points to the couch.

I stare at it for a moment, my mind wandering back to the hundreds of times I sat on that same couch with Isaiah. Tears spring to my eyes again, and I rub my palms into them to stop the flow.

"Aw, peanut," my dad starts as he wraps his arm around my shoulder and urges me to sit down. "It gets easier. I promise."

I cry in my father's arms for what feels like forever, and when the tears subside, I take a few deep breaths and lean against the cushions. I glance at him out of the corner of my eye.

"I know you don't like Isaiah, bu—"

"It has nothing to do with liking him, Tillie," he interrupts. "I love Isaiah. I've watched that boy grow up. Both him and Isabelle. It's just..."

"Just what Dad?"

"No one is ever going to be good enough for you." Dad sighs and leans back next to me. "And you both need to live a little before committing to forever."

I mull over his words and try to see things from his point of view. If my dad's taught me anything, it's to always try to look at things from all angles. Think, analyze, research, think some more.

"Have you given any more thought about college?" Dad breaks the silence and there's hope in his tone.

"Of course, I have." I shift on the couch so I'm facing him. "I'm gonna go, Dad. I'm just waiting to see where Isaiah's stationed. I want to be close to him."

Dad heaves a sigh of resignation. "Okay, Peanut." He rises to his feet and makes his way to the front door, pausing before opening it. "You've got your whole life ahead of you, Tillie. I just want you to be happy."

With those parting words, he leaves me alone with my thoughts. I keep circling back to the same thing, over and over again like a song on repeat.

Isaiah makes me happy.

1

ISAIAH

Seven years later...

"Sniper, rooftop, two o'clock."

The voice in my ear crackles through the military issue earpiece. I glance toward the roof up ahead and see the enemy Gordy warned me about. I take in our teammates, Philip, Seth, and Bruno, and motion for them to go ahead of me. When we reach the end of the burned-out block, my headset crackles again.

"Another sniper, opposite side."

"Can you take them out?" I ask in return.

"You got it," Gordy replies.

If it weren't for the fact that I'm listening for the muffled pop of his weapon, I'd never have known a gun was fired. Two bodies drop from rooftops. Philip checks the one on the right and Seth the one on the left. Bruno and I shuffle past them, not wanting to waste any more time getting to our target.

When we reach the edge of the relatively abandoned

town, I know we're getting closer. Our instructions had been to find Amal Hildebrah and capture him for questioning. He is suspected of running the foreign operations of a human trafficking ring.

This assignment was first brought to my attention a little over a year ago and I've put in the work to ensure my Seal team was the one chosen to execute the mission. We trained for months, researched the hell out of the files, and key players in the ring, and I'm not ashamed to admit, I had a few strings pulled.

"We're clear." Bruno's voice pulls me from my thoughts.

I look around at our surroundings to double check. Not because I don't trust my team but rather because we've been trained to always verify. Seeing that Bruno is right, I lower my weapon to my side and relax a little.

"Nice work, guys," I say to the four men who have had my back since day one in BUD/S training. I pull out the crude map we were given by an informant to make sure we're on the right track. "Looks like we've got about a three-mile walk to get to his last known location."

"Jesus, why ya gotta always get us involved in missions where we gotta walk?" Philip complains. The man is as fit as anyone I've ever seen but he likes to complain like a little bitch. If I didn't know him as well as I do, I'd probably hate him. But I know his complaints are just his way of lightening the mood.

"Have to find some way to walk off all the bread you eat from all the female admirers in every damn village," I joke.

"You got a problem with bread?"

"No. I can just think of better ways to spend time with the ladies than breaking bread."

"Yeah you can," Seth chimes in. "What was the name of that chick last week? Jane?"

"Shannon. Her name was Shannon." I chuckle and rub the side of my nose with a gloved hand. "At least, I think that was her name."

"Man, you really need to start remembering their names." Bruno slaps me on the back. "Take it from me, women treat you better when you call them by the right name. Call 'em by the wrong one and you're liable to get a severe case of blue balls."

I shake my head at them because I can't say what I want to say. That there is only one woman whose name I care to remember. An image of the blonde-haired beauty flashes through my mind and I push it away. Now is not the time to be thinking about her and all of the shoulda, coulda, wouldas that go along with those thoughts.

I let the guys get a bit ahead of me like I always do. I'm the team leader and while some would say that means I should be at the head of the line, I don't work that way. I have their backs. I fall back so I can make sure that there is no threat coming from behind.

I pull out the GPS again to check the remaining distance. When I glance down for the few seconds it takes to do that, the ground shakes and an explosion rips me off my feet and tosses me through the air like a rag doll.

Air whooshes from my lungs when I land in the packed dirt and pain radiates through my ribs as a rock digs into my side. My head bounces off the ground and smoke obscures my vision.

"Seth!" I shout, hoping to get a response. "Gordy, Philip, Bruno!"

Coughs wrack my body and I fight through the agony it causes. My ears are ringing, making it impossible to tell if the guys are responding. I rub my palms over my eyes to clear my vision and when it doesn't help, I start calling out to my team again. The ringing starts to dissipate and panic sets in when my yells go unreturned.

Get a grip, Isaiah. You're trained for this. Don't fucking panic.

I manage to get to my knees and push myself up to my feet. I sway a little and stretch my arms out to gain my balance. The smoke starts to die down and the dust from the blast settles. That's when I see the ball of fire created by what has to have been a bomb. I raise my gun with unsteady hands and turn in circles to evaluate for any threats.

I'm alone on the side of the road. There are no other people, no cars, no nothing. Just me, the flames and the intense heat. I get as close to the fire as I can but I'm not able to make out any bodies. Squinting, I make my way around the blast zone, looking for any sign of where my teammates are.

I don't see the body until it's almost too late. Bruno is on his back, almost unrecognizable with the amount of damage to his face. I swallow the bile that rises up the back of my throat and bend down to feel for a pulse. His skin is hot, almost too hot to touch, but I do it anyway. Nothing.

Seth, Philip, and Gordy are splayed out several hundred feet from Bruno and none of them have a pulse, either. I reach in my rucksack and pull out the radio to call for help. When my fingers wrap around the communication device, I can tell without even looking that it's busted, useless.

I tip my head back and stare at the sky. The bright blue expanse is free of clouds and is a stark contrast to the devastation around me. Inhaling, I review my options. I can head back to the abandoned town and pray that someone comes along or I can make my way to the original extraction point.

It's an easy decision. I have to get to the extraction point. I don't seem to have any broken limbs so the walk itself won't be difficult, but I have several busted ribs and the adrenaline is wearing off, making it very clear that my body hurts in ways I didn't think possible.

There's only one thing left to figure out... how the fuck am I going to get my men to the extraction point? Because if there's anything I've learned over the last seven years, it's that we leave no man behind.

2

TILLIE

"How do you want to celebrate?"

The letter in my hand is what I've been waiting for, the validation that hard work and sacrifice pays off. I read through the words again, making sure I got it right the first time. Holy shit! I passed. I busted my ass, breezed through the classes, put in hundreds of hours of studying, and gave a hundred and ten percent to my internship. And it wasn't all for nothing.

"Tillie?"

I glance to my right and take in Isabelle's questioning look. Tears well up in my eyes and I blink them back. I hate that I can't tell if they're from sadness or elation. Probably a little bit of both.

"I'm great."

"Bullshit." Isabelle reaches out and takes the letter from me. "Girl, you just found out you passed the bar exam. Why are you about to cry?"

I never was any good at lying to her. She knows me better than I know myself and almost better than her brother once knew me. But that was a long time ago.

I stand from the couch and Isabelle follows me to the kitchen. I pull out the Tequila from the cabinet and grab two shot glasses.

"Well, we're drinking, so that's a step in the right direction." She sets the letter on my kitchen table and steps next to me to lean against the counter. "C'mon, talk to me."

"The one person I want to tell about this, I can't." The second the words are out, I want to call them back. I pour the shots and hand her one. "To passing the bar exam."

We click glasses and down the liquor. I savor the burn as it glides down my throat and warms a path to my stomach. I quickly throw back two more shots before slamming the glass on the counter.

"You know you can write to him, right?" Isabelle's eyes seek out mine. "I know he'd love to—"

"You mean like he's written me?" I snap. "Because I don't recall a single letter, phone call, or text in seven years."

"Tillie, Isaiah—"

"Don't." I turn away from her and pour myself another shot. "I get that he's your brother and I don't even blame you for trying to defend him. But not today." I down the fiery liquid. "You're right, we need to celebrate. This is a good start but it's not gonna cut it." I nod toward the Tequila bottles. "Let's get outta here and hit up a few bars."

Isabelle raises a brow as if to question my seriousness. When she sees that I'm standing my ground, her features relax, and she nods. "Okay, let's go."

I glance down at myself and take in the jeans and hoodie I'm wearing and realize that I need to change first. Isabelle, as always, looks great, but I look like a bum. With reassurance to Isabelle that I'll 'be right back', I take twenty minutes to put on something a little more flattering and minimal makeup.

When I return to the living room, Isabelle is on her phone

and I can tell by her conversation that she's talking to Liam. She looks at me, quickly ends the call, and shoves her phone in her purse.

"Liam's gonna meet us at that place on Sixth Ave in Indy. We figure we should go someplace a little nicer than Dusty's for this celebration."

Dusty's is the dive bar we always go to and it's much closer to home but they're right, Dusty's isn't where I want to go. I don't give a shit about how run down it is or that another bar is more upscale. I do care that Dusty's will only remind me of who *isn't* here, and I don't need any more of that tonight.

"Sounds good," I reply and snag my keys off of the console table by the front door. "Do you mind if we take the bikes?"

"Not at all. We can always call an Uber if we can't drive home and have someone take us to get the bikes in the morning."

It takes longer than I would have liked to get to the bar, but I don't let that stop me from trying to have a good time. When we walk through the door and enter the dimly lit space, Liam is already at the bar and he makes his way to me, weaving in and out of the mingling bodies. He throws his arms around me and spins me in a circle before setting me on my feet and kissing my cheek.

"I'm so proud of you," he beams. "We've got a bonafide lawyer in the family."

Liam and I aren't blood family. But we are family… club family, and sometimes that's even better.

"Thanks." I smile at him. "Took a while but it was worth it."

"Did I hear someone say you're a lawyer?"

I whirl toward the voice and instantly recognize the new prosecutor. He's holding a tumbler with amber liquid and ice, swirling it around expertly. His white dress shirt is open at the collar and his black dress pants fit him perfectly. He's not my type but there's no denying that he's good looking, in a preppy, professional sort of way.

"Mr. Stringer, it's nice to see you." I take a sip of the drink that Isabelle hands me.

"Please, call me Henry." He takes a step toward me, closing the distance between us. "It's Tillie, right?"

"That's right," I confirm. We don't know each other well but during my internship, I'd see him in the office, and I've watched him in the courtroom. He's a prosecuting genius.

"So, did I hear right? You're a lawyer?"

"I passed the bar. If that makes me a lawyer then yes, I'm a lawyer." I give him a cheeky grin as the effects of the alcohol start to hit me.

"That's great. Definitely something to celebrate." Mr. Stringer—Henry—wraps his fingers around my elbow in a caressing manner. "Let me buy you a congratulatory drink."

He guides me to the bar, and I hear Isabelle and Liam cracking jokes behind us. Apparently, they think I need to let 'Mr. Prosecutor' take me home for a 'good time'. I swallow back the laughter that bubbles up my throat. That's not gonna happen. Maybe five or six years ago I wouldn't have thought twice about the possibility of a one-night stand, but I've fought too hard to bury that emotionless, broken girl. I'm better than that.

Four shots of Tequila and two Long Island Iced Teas later, I prove myself wrong. With enough booze, that girl rears her ugly head and enjoys a sinful night on silk sheets, wrapped in the arms of 'Mr. Prosecutor'.

3

ISAIAH

One year later...

Thwap... thwap... thwap...

The helicopter rotor blades pick up speed as we ascend into the sky for the last leg of my journey home. I stare out the window, ignoring the voices in the headset provided to me. I've been on hundreds of aircraft and no longer feel the rush of adrenaline I used to associate with it.

I clench and unclench my fists in my lap, a sense of dread taking over my ability to enjoy the scenery. It's been a long time since I've been home, too long. I've dreamt of this day over and over and over again, always picturing open arms, happy tears and a sense of accomplishment that only being a Navy Seal could provide. Instead, I know I'm going to get worried glances, a ton of fucking questions, and probably a tongue lashing from the one person I want to see the most.

"Do you have someone picking you up, Chief?"

I shake my head without looking at the pilot. My dad is the only one who knows I'm coming home. At least, he's the only one I told. After months of sitting on some head shrinkers couch, I gave up on getting over the cluster fuck of my last mission and called him. He, more than anyone understands what I'm going through. He wanted answers to questions I wasn't ready for, so instead of giving them, I asked him to drop off my bike at the local airstrip. Most of my belongings are being shipped home so everything I have on me can fit into my saddlebags.

"Ten more minutes, Chief."

"It's just Isaiah," I snap, frustrated at his use of my military title.

I'm not a Navy Seal. I'm nothing but a veteran with PTSD who was found to no longer be fit to serve my country. I should be grateful that I'm going home, especially when so many of my team were returned to their families in body bags. The bombing that ended my career, ended their *lives*.

"Right. Sorry," the pilot mumbles.

I glance at him out of the corner of my eye. He looks older than my twenty-six years, but that means nothing to me. I've seen more, *done* more, than most people my age. And once I dive into the MC my father built, the Broken Rebel Brotherhood, those things will only increase in number.

I reach into my bag and pull out the letter I received from my mom. I skim the words and my eyes are drawn to the same six they have been for the last week: risk of having a heart attack. She's referring to my dad and it's such a hard concept to wrap my brain around. The man that raised me, started the MC, is a veteran, former Navy Seal, the epitome of everything strong. The same man who has always seemed larger than life is not as healthy as he wants everyone to believe.

He's in his sixties, Isaiah. He's getting older.

In the letter, she explains that dad has been having problems for several months and I can't help but wonder if all the shit I unloaded on him contributed to the issues. Did I cause this, make it worse? Should I have kept my own crap to myself?

I crumble the letter in my fist and refocus my attention to what's beyond the window. The landscape is the same as I remember… flat. Indiana isn't a mountainous state, but if you like fields and rural towns, it's perfect.

As the helicopter descends, I spot my Harley Fat Bob in the corner of the lot. The black and red custom paint job gleams in the sunlight, and I breathe a sigh of relief that my dad listened and didn't stick around to greet me. A rush of guilt also hits for asking him to do anything for me when he's got so much on his plate.

The landing is smooth, a testament to the skills of the pilot. I take the headset off and set it on the dash before opening the door and stepping out of the aircraft. When my feet touch solid ground, I shake my legs to regain some feeling. Being cramped for any length of time is difficult with my 6'4" frame, but it's worse since the bombing.

"Thanks for the lift." I shake the pilot's hand before grabbing my duffel.

"Anytime."

He turns his back on me and begins his post-flight check. Throwing my bag over my shoulder, I pivot and stare at my Harley for a few moments before trudging in that direction. The closer I get to the steel beast, the closer to the ground my stomach gets.

When I reach Nyx, my Harley, I toss my stuff into the saddlebag and palm the key my dad left in there for me. I straddle Nyx and before I sit, I pull my cell phone out of my pocket.

Motherfucker!

Nine missed calls and fourteen texts, all of which are from the members of the Broken Rebel Brotherhood who naturally became my family as I grew up. *So, Dad didn't keep his mouth shut.* I take note of the fact that there's one person who didn't call, didn't text. And that only serves to twist my insides.

Just as I'm about to pull off, my cell vibrates and, with a quick glance at the name on the screen, I hit the green icon and answer.

"Couldn't keep your mouth shut, could ya, Pops?"

"No, he couldn't." The soothing voice of my mother comes through the line. "And he shouldn't have had to. You couldn't even be bothered to call your mother?"

"Jesus," I mumble under my breath.

"Watch your mouth." Mom chastises me as if I'm twelve and not a grown-ass man who was a Navy Seal for eight years and has seen the worst of the worst this world has to offer.

Ignoring her frustration, I say, "So Pops told everyone, huh?"

"You know your father. He's happy you're going to be home." I hear noise in the background and no doubt my dad is near. Unless my dad is on a club mission, he's never far from his 'Sweetness' as he calls her. "We all are." There's a heaviness to her tone and I can't help but think she's referring to the information in her letter.

Shoving that thought far out of my head, I respond with words that I can't stop. "I can think of at least one person who won't be happy to see me."

"About that..."

"Not now, mom."

"Isaiah, there are a few—"

"Please." I know cutting her off is going to piss her off, but I can't think about *her* just yet. "I'll be home soon. We'll talk then."

"Okay."

I hear the disappointment in her voice, mixed in with a

bit of frustration, but I ignore it. She'll forget all about it the second I walk into the house. That's how it's always worked with my mom. She never could stay mad at me or my twin sister, Isabelle.

I end the call and shove my phone back in my pocket before starting Nyx and pointing her in the direction of home. *Home.* I tried to mentally prepare myself for this day, but I certainly didn't expect it to happen like this. I thought when I left the Seals, it'd be my decision, not some doctors.

Within twenty-five minutes, I'm slowing down and pulling through the front gates of the property. My cramped muscles begin to unwind, and by the time I park in front of my parent's house, I'm more relaxed than I've been in eight years. Eight fucking years.

"Isaiah!"

I swing my leg over Nyx in time to catch a flying Isabelle as she launches herself into my arms. She's filled out since I last saw her at eighteen. When I set her on her feet, I am struck by how much I've missed her.

"You went and grew up, Izzy."

"Ah, bro, we're the same age. Like, the exact same age." She laughs but it's short-lived before she sobers. "Maybe if you came home once in a while, it wouldn't be such a shock."

And there's the sister I know and love. Attitude from hell and so full of life that I have no idea how we're twins.

"Don't start, Izzy," I warn with a bite to my tone. "It's been a long day and I just want to come in and say 'hi' to the parentals and grab some shut-eye."

Isabelle shifts her gaze in the direction of the main house, the one where church is held and where prospects reside until they have a cabin built. When her eyes meet mine again, I know she's hiding something.

"Spit it out, Iz," I snap.

"Dad's at the main house." She crosses her arms over her chest in a defensive move that mirrors my own.

"Mom told me about his health problems." Her eyes burn with fire, probably mistakenly thinking that I talked to mom and not her. But there's also another look there, one that says dad's health is not what she was thinking about. "And..." I drag the word out.

"And nothing." She shrugs and lets her arms fall to her sides. "He said he wanted to see you when you got here."

I heave a sigh. I just spent eight years being ordered around, and apparently, there's no escaping it. *He's your president, too, dumbass. Of course, you're going to be ordered around.*

"Fine." I look toward the front porch, noticing it's empty for the first time. "Where's Mom?"

"She's at the main house, too."

"Damn. Must be something big if they're both there."

"You could say that."

I narrow my eyes at her cryptic statement but can tell by her pursed lips that I won't get any further explanation. I swing my leg back over Nyx and prepare to head to the main house. I glance back at Izzy over my shoulder and smile.

"Wanna ride with me?"

Isabelle has her own Harley, and I know she'd prefer to be on it, but she never could pass up a ride with her brother. At least, not eight years ago. Her eyes light up and she makes quick work of climbing on behind me. Her hands settle on my sides, and I drive slower than normal with her back there.

It takes no more than five minutes to reach the main house. When I park Nyx and lower the kickstand, Isabelle hops off and runs up the steps, and disappears inside. I glance around at the bikes already here. There are six bikes in total, but only one stands out. It's a teal and black Harley

Street Glide that I would recognize anywhere. The black Mercedes parked next to it is equally hard to miss.

I trudge inside and am instantly greeted by the sounds, smells, and feelings of my childhood. Grease, leather, loyalty, family, service, passion. The Broken Rebel Brotherhood was started by my father and his Navy Seal team when they were all discharged from the military. The motorcycle club was their way of finding meaning and purpose in their lives when nothing made sense. Isabelle and I were teethed on the club's mantra: Protect those who can't protect themselves.

I make my way through the main living room and down the hall to the library, where church is held and where I know my parents will be. With each step I take, my heart pounds faster, my stomach knots further. When I reach the doors, I take a deep breath and grab the handle. Before I can turn the knob, the door swings open and my jaw drops.

Wide blue eyes stare back at me in shock. My mouth goes dry and my brain seems to shut down. Words are impossible, as is any coherent thought. I don't even register what's happening until a tiny fist connects with my cheek and my head flies sideways.

I shake off the pain, both physical and emotional, and glare at the pissed off woman in front of me. Finally, the cobwebs clear and I manage to form a smile, even if it's only to taunt her.

"Nice to see you too, Tillie."

4

TILLIE

"What? Nothing to say?"

Isaiah's scowl deepens, as does the mark on his cheek my fist left behind. It felt good to punch him, although it did nothing to erase eight years of hatred, of bitterness. I cross my arms over my chest and glare back at him, praying he wilts under my stare. He doesn't.

I whirl around and run straight into my boyfriend, who's dressed in a suit tailored to fit him perfectly and stumble backward a few steps. My eyes focus on Henry's face as he reaches out to steady me, but it's the scorching heat from Isaiah's hands on my back that cause me to stay unbalanced.

"Honey, are you okay?"

The concern in Henry's tone sets my teeth on edge. I check the impulse to punch him in the face, too, and beam a smile.

"I'm fine, thanks," I reply in a sugary sweet tone.

"Good, good." He bobs his head and then I track his gaze to the behemoth of a man behind me. "Are you going to introduce me?"

"Yeah, *Peanut,* are you going to introduce us?"

My entire body tenses at Isaiah's use of my nickname and his condescending tone. I will my muscles to uncoil and when I trust myself not to cause bodily harm to either of them, I step to the side and turn so I can see both of them.

"Henry, this is Isaiah." I glance at the asshole who tossed me aside like so much trash. "He's… Micah's son. Isaiah," I nod toward the man who now warms my bed. "This is Henry. My boyfriend."

I take great satisfaction in the way Isaiah's jaw clenches and his body stiffens at the news. He shoves his hands in his pockets and I can see the outline of his fists tightening beneath the fabric.

"It's nice to finally meet you." Henry thrusts his hand in Isaiah's direction, but Isaiah ignores it. "I have to say, I've heard a lot of stories. Seems I'm in the presence of a true hero."

"I'm nobody's hero," Isaiah barks.

"Got that right," I mumble.

Isaiah narrows his eyes at me before clearing his throat and stepping around me to go to his parents. I turn and watch as the three embrace each other, clearly happy to have the family together again. My eyes burn at the scene before me, and I take a deep breath and manage to stop the tears from welling and spilling over my lashes.

"Tillie, honey, what's wrong?"

Henry rests his hand on my forearm, and I shake it off, instantly regretting the action when I catch the hurt that flashes in his brown eyes. His average, *boring* brown eyes. I loop my arm through his and pull him to me for a quick peck.

"I'm sorry." I mean it, too. I *am* sorry. Just not for what he thinks. I rub my forehead in an attempt to ease the migraine that's threatening to take hold. "I'm just not feeling very well. Maybe I should head home and call it a day."

"Tomorrow's a big day," he reminds me, unnecessarily. "Maybe you should get some rest. We can't afford for you to be off your game during the hearing."

"He's right, Til." I whip my head in the direction of Micah, my surrogate uncle and president of the Broken Rebel Brotherhood. "Let's get Isaiah caught up really quick and then you can go."

I nod in agreement. That is the reason Isaiah is here after all. He certainly didn't come to the main house to see me.

"Pops, I know I need to be pulled into the loop, but I'm beat. Can't this wait a few days? At least until I get settled in."

My eyes seek out Isaiah, willingly this time. That's when I notice that there are lines on his face that make him look far more worldly than he should at twenty-six. Hell, I've got the same damn lines. The ones that tell everyone we come into contact with that we've seen things, bad things.

When Micah doesn't respond, I roll my eyes and huff out a breath. "No, it can't wait." I face Isaiah and ignore the way my heart skips a beat. "I know I'm the last person you want to deal with, but you came home at the perfect time. We need all the muscle we can get."

"What the fuck are you talking about?"

"Isaiah!" Sadie chastises. I manage to hold back a snort at the chagrin on his face. "You two can work out your shit later. Right now, we've got work to do."

Isaiah doesn't respond to his mom as he strides toward the head of the long table that has long since replaced the couch that used to be in this room. Micah clears his throat at his spot being taken, and Isaiah shifts to the side and crosses his muscled and tatted arms across his very broad chest. I swallow past the lump in my throat at the way his Henley hugs his frame, allowing for maximum definition of every sinful inch.

"Tillie, can you go grab your dad, Griff, and Brie?" Micah

asks me. He pauses and rubs a hand over his chest, something he's been doing a lot lately. "And tell Isabelle she can quit listening from just outside the door and come in." The last part he says loud enough for her to hear, and I can't stop the laugh that escapes when she slinks through the door.

I go to do his bidding, bumping Izzy's shoulder as I pass her. I make quick work of gathering everyone because genuine fear creeps in at the thought of Henry and Isaiah being in a room together. Henry knows about my past with Isaiah, but only what I've told him, and lord only knows what Isaiah thinks of my choice in men.

When I return to the library, Isaiah and Henry are seated across from one another at the table, and Micah is seated at the head of the table with his wife, Sadie, next to him. It's always been that way with the Brotherhood. Not only are women cherished, they're included in decision making.

It takes a few minutes for Isaiah to be welcomed home by those who just joined us, but when it's done, the vibe of the room turns somber, serious. No more hugging, no more back-slapping, or 'how the hell have you beens'. Just an electric-charged quiet. When I can't take it any longer, I face Isaiah and resign myself to being the one to explain things to him.

"I have a client who was raped by her husband." I cross my arms and continue to stand behind my chair. "Henry is the prosecuting attorney for the state and the trial is tomorrow."

Isaiah takes advantage of my pause. "Client?" He arches a brow.

"Yes, client," I snap, losing control of my temper. "I'm a lawyer. You'd know that if you ever bothered to come home, write, call... anything!"

A hand settles on my arm, and I spare a glance to see who it's attached to. Henry. As much as I want to shake him off, to make him let me release eight fucking years of pent up rage, I don't.

"At least now the fancy car parked out front makes sense," Isaiah taunts, smirking at Henry.

"Listen, asshole, you don't get to come home and—"

"Enough!" Micah barks, slamming a fist on the table and rattling anything and everything sitting atop it. When all eyes turn to him, he takes a deep breath and rubs his chest again. He focuses his attention on his son. "Isaiah, you've been gone for a long time. I respected your wishes and let you do what you felt you needed to do, but now you're home. And we've got work to do." His eyes cut to me. "Tillie, you're pissed off, hurt, feeling betrayed. I get that. But now is not the time. We need to make sure we've got tomorrow covered. Torture each other on your own time."

I yank my chair out and sit down with more force than necessary. Isaiah does the same and we continue to stare each other down. Seems that's going to be a common occurrence for a while.

Micah spends the next ten minutes recapping his meeting with the sheriff earlier today to organize security efforts. The Brotherhood has always worked with law enforcement, and that relationship only gets stronger as the years go by.

"Basically, I need to be there tomorrow and stick close to the wife," Isaiah confirms with his father. I somehow managed to get pulled into my thoughts and missed most of what was said so I refocus my attention.

"We want the husband to know she's got backup. He's a vindictive bastard, and there's concern about what he'll do to her in retaliation for her testimony against him, if he's not convicted."

Isaiah seems to mull over the information, and his face hardens. He always has been a sucker for anyone in need. It's in his blood and it's not something he can ignore. Ever. That quality is one of the things I love—correction, *loved* —about him.

"Do you think you can stick around long enough to see this through tomorrow?" I ask with a massive amount of sass.

"Oh, I can stick around," he mocks. "I'll stick so close, you'll be begging me to leave again."

Henry's hand tightens on my arm, and I realize he never removed it. "You don't need to stick close to Tillie. She's a big girl and can take care of herself." Henry's tone is the most threatening I've ever heard, but still, it's no match for Isaiah.

"Are we done here?" Isaiah asks his dad as he rises from his chair and turns his back on everyone else in the room, on me.

"We're done," Micah responds and stands, swaying a bit on his feet.

As I track Isaiah's movement across the room toward the door, my heart pounds in my chest and every single negative emotion swirls in my head.

Done here?

Hardly.

We haven't even started.

Just as the door opens, a thud reaches my ears, along with the echoed scream of Sadie.

"Micah!"

5

ISAIAH

For as long as I live, I'll never forget that scream. I'll never forget the way my head spun as I whirled around toward the sound and took in the sight of my dad lying on the floor. I'll never forget the flashes of memory that assaulted me, making it almost impossible for me to move, the other men I saw on their backs, unmoving. I'll never forget the way my world seemed to stop spinning for a second time and the look of pure terror on my mom and sister's faces.

The flurry of activity pulls me from my paralyzed state, and I rush to my dad's side, drop to my knees and shake him. "Dad?" No response. "Pops, c'mon, wake up!" I shout. Nothing. "Someone call 911," I bark over my shoulder.

My mom is kneeling on the other side of my dad, mumbling incoherently with tears streaming down her cheeks. I have no idea how much time passes before I'm being pulled away from him as paramedics move in to do their jobs. I scrub my hands over my face, feeling the weight of the world crashing around me.

My mom stays with my dad, holding his hand, as he's

hauled away on a stretcher, his face pale and ashen. A large hand rests on my shoulder, startling me.

"Why don't you ride with us to the hospital?" I look into the eyes of Griffin and see a concern, a fear, that mirrors my own.

"Thanks, but…" I take a deep breath and release it in a rush. I feel twitchy, on edge, *not* in the mood to be cooped up in a vehicle with anyone. "I've got my bike."

I start to walk away and am stopped in my tracks by a hand gripping my arm. I drop my gaze to the slender fingers and my gut twists. I raise my head and glare at Tillie. "Isaiah, I'm—"

I yank my arm out of her hold and walk away, my stride long and angry. My boots echo on the hardwood floor as I make my way to the front door. When I reach my bike, I start her up and take off toward the hospital.

The wind whips my face as I ride. It's cold and unforgiving, matching my attitude perfectly. My knuckles ache as my grip on the handlebars tightens. I try to relax, let the freedom of my bike lull me into a sense of calm, but it's impossible. How can I relax when everything is on the verge of crumbling to the ground? How can I relax when I might lose my dad so soon after losing my men? How?

I pull into the hospital parking lot and am off my bike so fast it almost tips over. The fact that I almost let it, tells me just how fried my nerves are. I stride through the glass doors of the emergency department and head straight toward the others already in the waiting room.

"Any news?" I ask Isabelle, who's wrapped her arms around herself and is pacing the linoleum floor.

She shakes her head. "He's awake, but they're running some tests."

"Fuck!" I yell, at no one in particular, and all eyes turn toward me.

I shove my fingers through my short hair and start to pace. The minutes tick by and turn into hours as I listen to everyone speculate as to whether or not Pops had a heart attack.

"Is there an Isaiah and Isabelle here?"

I stop in my tracks and look at the doctor who just called our names. He looks somber and my heart plummets.

"I'm Isaiah," I say and stick out my hand to shake his. "How is he?" Isabelle stands next to me, her arm looped through mine.

"He's going to be okay. He's asking for you both." The doctor turns away from me. "I'll let you talk with him for a few minutes and then I'll come in and review everything with you all."

We follow the doctor to the emergency bay where my father is. He pulls the curtain back and I take a deep breath to prepare myself for what I'm going to see. I'm shocked when I see Pops sitting up in bed, more color in his cheeks, and a smile on his face. My mom is sitting in a chair next to the bed with her hand firmly gripping his, almost as if she's afraid to let go for fear that he'll disappear if she does.

"Hey Pops," I say, trying to inject a lightness into my tone that I don't feel.

"Daddy," Isabelle cries as she rushes to his side.

"Baby girl, don't cry." Dad wraps his free arm around her and drops a kiss to the top of her head. "I'm fine."

Isabelle stands up and glances at me for a moment before returning her gaze to the man in the bed. "What happened?" she asks.

"Just a little case of angina. I'll be fine." Our dad smiles at both of us and then at our mom. "I'm even going to be coming home today. As soon as the damn doctors give me discharge instructions."

"Are you sure going home is a good idea?" I ask, unable to get the image of him lying on the floor out of my head.

"I do." My dad holds my stare. "A few things will need to change but I'll be fine."

"What has to change?" I arch a brow. So much has already changed. I don't know that I can handle anything else.

Before my dad can answer, the curtain is pulled open and the doctor steps in. He reads from the iPad in his hand which I can only assume is the hospital's electronic filing system. When he looks up, his expression is more reassuring than it was when he came to retrieve us from the waiting room.

"Okay, Mr. Mallory, there are a few things I want to go over before I can discharge you."

"Hit me, Doc."

The doctor clears his throat. "As I told you earlier, what you experienced is angina. It can mimic a heart attack but is less dangerous. That being said, your tests indicate that you are at risk for a heart attack, or even a stroke." He pushes his glasses up his nose with his index finger.

"A heart attack?" My mom's hand flies to her mouth. "How do we prevent that from happening?"

"There are several things you can do to mitigate the risk." He pauses to hand my mom a packet of paperwork. "Everything is outlined there. The two biggest factors I want you to focus on right now are diet and stress. Improve one and reduce the other."

"Doc, I don't know if you're aware, but stress kind of comes with the territory in my line of work."

"Micah, I've been around long enough to know exactly what your 'line of work' entails. But, you're not a young man anymore. You're in your sixties and it's time for you to slow down a bit."

"Maybe it's time to pass the reigns." My mom's voice is quiet, but there's an authority to it that's impossible to miss.

"Mom's right," Isabelle chimes in. "Isaiah's home now and can take over."

My head spins at the thought of stepping into my father's shoes as President of the club. Granted, I knew it would happen eventually, but I wasn't expecting it less than twenty-four hours after getting home.

You weren't expecting Pops to be in the ER either.

"Whatever you decide to do," the doctor interrupts. "The stress level has to come down. Unless you want to be in here for a much longer stay or in the morgue, that's non-negotiable."

"We'll discuss this when we get home," Pops concedes. "With the rest of the club."

I sigh, feeling like a reprieve was just granted. No way will the rest of the club agree to this. Not when I've been gone so long and there are other options, other members to get the job done.

"As soon as you sign the paperwork, you're free to go." The doctor hands him the iPad and dad signs some forms with the attached pen. "Your copies will be at the front desk for you. We've also scheduled a follow-up with a cardiologist so you can start receiving routine care."

Pops grumbles but ultimately agrees to go to the appointment. Isabelle and I step back out into the waiting room and are peppered with questions. We answer what we can and let everyone know that there'll be a meeting with voting members later in the evening after Pops is settled.

When I leave the hospital, new worries trickle in, new fears and insecurities. What if I am voted in as President?

Fuck, what if I'm not?

When I walk into the library, there are more faces than there were at the earlier meeting. Most I recognize but a few are new. Liam, Griffin and Brie's son, and one of my best friends, strides toward me with a wide smile spreading across his face. He throws his arms around me and lifts me up into a giant bear hug.

"Damn, man, it's so good to see you."

I return the hug, probably longer than necessary in light of recent events. "I've missed you too."

"We're gonna need to catch up soon. Maybe hit up Dusty's?"

"Sounds good, brother."

"Hey, there are a few guys I want to introduce you to before things get underway." Liam turns toward three men standing just behind him. "Isaiah, this is Jace, Noah, and Adam. Guys, this is Isaiah, Micah and Sadie's son."

"Nice to meet you," Noah says as he shakes my hand. "Heard a lot about you."

"You too," I respond. "What branch did you serve in?"

"Army," Noah says.

"Air Force." Both Jace and Adam speak at once.

"You're a Seal, right?" Adam asks.

"Let's get this meeting started."

My dad's booming voice saves me from having to answer that question and the litany of questions that were sure to follow.

"As you all know, I've had a bit of a health scare," Pops starts. "And at the doctor's recommendation, have decided to make some changes." He looks to Griffin, his right-hand man, his VP. "Care to kick things off?"

Griffin stands, as do Aiden and the rest of the members. "Members of the Broken Rebel Brotherhood, we've built something to be proud of." Griffin smiles but it's a sad smile. Brie, my mom, and Scarlett all wipe tears from their eyes.

"When Micah called on all of us over twenty years ago, I don't think a single one of us ever expected to be where we are today. We've increased in numbers, built new chapters, helped hundreds of people who couldn't help themselves. Not only our clients but our members, our prospects, our *families*." Griffin takes a deep breath and cuts his stare to me. "But, it's time for some new blood to take over the reins. We all love what we do and while we aren't going anywhere, it's time we all step down. I'd like to nominate Isaiah Mallory as the new president of the Broken Rebel Brotherhood. All those in favor, let your vote be known."

With wide eyes and a pounding heart, I listen as, one by one, every person at the table votes 'yes'. Every. Single. Person. By the time the vote is over, my own eyes aren't dry. My parents are standing behind me, each with a hand on one of my shoulders.

This is what I want, what I've always wanted, but not like this. Not on the heels of an almost tragedy. And I always thought I'd have a certain blue-eyed blonde at my side.

"Well, son," my dad starts. "The BRB is your baby now. Do me proud."

"I will, Pops." I swipe at the wetness on my cheeks. "I promise." I take a deep breath and look at Liam. "I'd like to nominate Liam as VP." I glance around the room. "All those in favor, let your vote be known."

Again, a chorus of yes's all around. The next ten minutes are spent voting on the rest of the members and congratulatory hugs and back slaps.

"You may want to take your rightful place." Isabelle nods toward the head of the table, to the seat that has always been my dad's.

I make my way around the room to do just that. It feels foreign to stand where he's stood for so many years. It's a heady feeling, knowing that I now hold all the power. But like my dad, I won't let that power go to my head. I won't let it get in the way of what must be done. I won't let it get in the way of the club, of the legacy, of my family.

"Can I say something?"

I glance at Tillie, who's sitting a few seats down from me with her arms crossed over her chest.

"Sure," I say, not convinced I want to hear what she's thinking but needing to just the same.

"I may have voted 'yes', but I need it to be known that I have concerns." Tillie stands and shoves her chair under the table. My shoulders tense and heat races through me. "You left once. What's to stop you from leaving again?"

"Tillie, this isn't the time—"

I hold my hand up to stop Aiden from speaking. "It's okay." I swallow down my anger. "She's right, I did leave." I rise to my feet. "But I left because I needed to earn my position in this club. I left because I had to. Now," I take a deep breath. "I'll stay because I have to keep earning my position and because I want to. I don't expect any of you to believe me, but I will prove to you that you made the right decision."

"You didn't need to leave!" Tillie shouts. "You *wanted* to. There's a big difference."

I look away from the rage in Tillie's eyes and focus on the rest of the voting members. "Do we have any other business to discuss?" When everyone shakes their heads 'no', I give a tight nod. "Meeting adjourned."

The sound of chairs scraping against the floor, of feet shuffling as everyone makes their way out of the room, barely registers. The only thing that's holding my attention is Tillie, who remains right where she was behind her chair. When it's just the two of us left, I stalk toward her.

"Don't you ever do that again," I snarl.

"Do what?" she taunts.

"I don't give a damn if you want to speak your mind, but

if you ever bring our personal shit to the table again, we're gonna have an issue. Got it?"

"Whatever."

Tillie whirls around to walk away from me but I grab her arm and halt her movement. Her chest is heaving, and her eyes are sparking fire.

"I'm here to stay, so you might as well get used to it."

"We'll see about that."

She yanks out of my hold and storms out of the library. I watch her retreating back and take a few deep breaths to calm my anger. When I hear the front door slam, I finally allow myself to move. I follow Tillie's path and pass Isabelle in the hallway, leaning against the wall.

"Isaiah?"

I ignore my sister and continue out of the house and down the front steps. I ignore Tillie's barely concealed mumbling from her spot in the chair on the porch.

"Where the fuck are you going?"

Isabelle's tone is harsh as I straddle Nyx and rev the engine. Being in the same room as Tillie, breathing the same air… my dad wasn't wrong. It was torture. Agonizing, soul-crushing, mind-fucking, *welcome* torture. But hearing her voice concerns that mimic my own is infuriating.

"Isaiah, don't do this. Don't go running off." Isabelle pleads with me from her position next to my bike.

"Give me one good reason why I shouldn't." I swing my head in her direction, meeting her eyes. "Iz, you may very well be the only person who fucking wants me here."

"That's not true and you know it. You were voted President, after all." She takes a step closer to me and pats my cheek. "It won't be tense forever. But you've gotta give her time."

"Time?" I balk. "Time isn't a luxury that we're guaranteed."

Isabelle sighs and steps back, crossing her arms over her chest. She stares off into the distance, appearing to get her thoughts under control.

"You've changed." Her tone is sad, resigned. "But you aren't the only one. Tillie was crushed when you didn't co—"

The sound of an engine pulls my attention away from Isabelle. My eyes narrow at the sight of the Mercedes that parks near the porch and the man that steps out of it. Tillie stands from the Adirondack chair and greets her fancy-pants boyfriend. Immediately, the sound of raised voices reaches my ears and Tillie's arms start flailing. Some things never change. Tillie will always have a temper, and you can tell just how fired up she is by how fast her hands and arms are moving.

I watch in fascination as Tillie goes from pissed off to calm, cool, and collected within minutes. *That's different.* Since when does she back down? Unable to take any more, I shake my head in disgust and spare a quick glance at Isabelle.

"I'm outta here."

"Isaiah, wai—"

Her voice is drowned out by the roar of the engine. Dust flies as I tear off down the driveway and back to my parents' house. I really need to find a place of my own because the last thing I need right now is a confrontation with my parents when they get home. Not only that, but my dad doesn't need my issues causing him more stress.

I make my way through the house and to my old room, slamming the door behind me. After tossing my duffel on the bed, I flop down beside it with my arms beneath my head and let my legs dangle over the edge.

The events of the last twenty-four hours, hell, the last year, catch up to me and I start to doze off.

"You know you don't have to do this, right?"

I look at my mom and hate the sadness I see in her eyes. Even more than that, I hate that I'm the reason for it.

"I have to, mom. You know as well as I do that if I ever want to take over as president of the Broken Rebel Brotherhood, I need to be worthy. I need to earn the title."

"You were born into the club, Isaiah. You have nothing to prove. None of you kids do."

"Every single member of the Brotherhood is a veteran," I argue. "You're scared, mom. I get it. But this is something I have to do."

"But you could be—"

"Sweetness, you ready to go?"

I give my dad a grateful look for interrupting when he did. If I had to continue the conversation, I'd cave, if for no other reason than to make my mom happy and all at the expense of my own happiness.

"I guess." Mom heaves a dramatic sigh before taking a step back and leaning into my dad's side. "Have you talked to Tillie about this?" she asks, twisting the knife a little bit more.

My stomach drops, as it always does when I think about how my choices are affecting Tillie. When I left eight weeks ago, I promised her we'd be together soon. And now? Well, now I'm going to BUD/S training to hopefully earn a spot with the Navy Seals.

"No." I shake my head. "I don't know how to—"

I'm jolted from my dreams by a loud banging noise. Instinctively, I reach for the weapon under my pillow and when my hand comes away empty, I remember that I'm back in Indiana and not on a military base in the middle of nowhere. I wasn't exactly having a nightmare, but the dream took me back to the start of a living one.

My heart is racing and sweat trickles down my forehead as I roll out of bed. Footsteps on the stairs cause the hair on the back of my neck to stand up, and I stealthily make my way to the door.

"Isaiah Thomas Mallory, you better be decent."

Tillie's voice registers at the same moment the door flies open, and I'm forced to jump out of the way so that a broken nose isn't added to the bruise she left earlier. There's no time to recover before she closes the distance between us and shoves me backward with two small hands on my chest.

"What the hell, Til?"

I wrap my fingers around her wrists to stop her assault. She struggles against my hold, but she barely manages to pull back an inch.

"It's Tillie, asshole. You lost the right to use any nicknames with me the moment you decided to stay gone." Her blue eyes spark fire, and, smart man that I am, I keep my mouth shut and release my grip because that's a sure sign that she's not even close to being done unleashing her rage. "You couldn't even be bothered to tell me your plans. You're a goddamn coward!"

"Don't," I growl, warning clear in my tone.

"Don't what?" she counters and takes a step back. "Don't call it like I see it? Have you fucking met me, Isaiah?"

"Oh, I've met you. *All* of you." I advance on her and lean in to whisper in her ear. "Or don't you remember all the ways we know each other?"

Tillie's body stiffens, and her eyes are wide when I straighten to look at her. Crimson stains her cheeks, and I know she's remembering. With what we had together, it's hard not to. Her shoulders slump, and she glances beyond me toward the window.

"I remember," she mumbles. "I tried like hell to forget you, but, unlike you, I can't forget." When her gaze returns to me, her eyes are shimmering. "What I *have* managed to do is figure out who I am without you. I'm good now. My life is good. *Henry* is—"

"Not your type."

Tillie's eyes narrow at the interruption but only for a split second. "You don't know what my type is. Not now. Hell, you don't even know who *I* am anymore."

I take a deep breath and hold it for a few moments, hoping like hell that she's done talking but bracing for the likelihood of her not being anywhere close to done.

"I've changed Isaiah." *Definitely not done.* "I'm not some pie-eyed teenager with a thing for her best friend's twin. I'm a grown-ass woman, a fucking lawyer for Christ's sake."

"Newsflash, Tillie. I'm not a teenager anymore either." I begin to pace, unable to contain the energy coursing through me. "Do you have any idea what I've been through in the last few months?" My booted feet thump on the hardwood floor with each step I take. "Never mind. I don't want to hear the answer to that. Fuck!"

Pain radiates through my knuckles the second they go through the wall next to the window. I stare out over the club's massive property and do my best to ignore the blood I feel dripping from my hand. The floorboards creak behind me and my body deflates.

Smooth, Isaiah. Scare Tillie. That'll win her over.

My conscience goes to war with itself, rehashing every moment since first seeing Tillie to my fist going through my bedroom wall. While I stand there and give myself a mental ass-chewing, my thoughts are cut short when something soft is wrapped around my fingers.

I look down and see Tillie holding a towel over the fresh wounds. She refuses to look at me while she does her best to stop the bleeding. Her nearness washes over me, and my muscles begin to relax. I slowly turn toward her and curl the fingers on my other hand around her wrist.

"It's okay," I say in a hushed tone. "Thanks."

Finally, she raises her eyes to mine, and for the first time in eight years, I see the reason I was able to keep going, keep fighting, keep *breathing*: Love.

"That's the one thing, the *only* thing, that's never changed, Isaiah."

"What?"

Her response makes me realize that I actually spoke the word 'love' out loud.

"I may hate you, but," she inhales deeply before continuing. "I never stopped loving you."

6

TILLIE

"Tillie, I love ya babe, but if you don't stop pacing, I'm gonna bitch slap you."

I glare at Isabelle until she sticks her tongue out at me in a move she knows will make me laugh. I try to stop the curve of my lips, but I can't. She makes it impossible to hold onto anger. Besides, it's not her fault her brother's a dick. It's not her fault that I see him every time I look at her. And it's certainly not her fault that I still love the damn man.

"C'mon," she urges and pats the bed beside her. "Sit down and talk to me."

I huff out a breath and take a few steps toward my bed before flopping down on the mattress next to her. I look around, and sadness washes over me. Seeing Isaiah takes me back to a place that I don't ever want to be in again. That place where a person questions their sanity, wonders if life is worth the pain. That place where a person knows beyond a shadow of a doubt that they'll never be whole again.

"How bad was he?" she asks.

Isabelle was on my front porch when I got home from seeing Isaiah at their parent's house. She was rocking in the chair, holding a pint of Ben and Jerry's ice cream and two plastic spoons. I would have preferred a bottle of wine over ice cream, but Isabelle knows I don't drink the night before a trial involving one of my clients, whether I'm one of the attorneys presenting a case or not.

"He was horrible." The words leave my mouth without me feeling an ounce of guilt for badmouthing her brother. We made a pact years ago that we could, and would, talk about anything, regardless of how uncomfortable it may be. I sigh. "He was pitiful."

"Horrible, I can believe." She chuckles. "But pitiful? I think I need more info because that doesn't sound like my brother."

"I don't even know how to explain it. He was angry, for sure, but there was something else. Something more." I think back over my conversation—okay, argument—and one detail sticks out. "He said something about what he's gone through in the last few months." I turn my head to look at my friend. "Any idea what he was talking about?"

When she looks away from me, I sit up so fast my head spins.

"Isabelle Renee Mallory, don't you dare try to lie to me."

The use of her full name has a similar effect as it did on Isaiah. Her body stiffens for a split second, but she quickly relaxes. She knows she's been caught. No point in trying to lie.

"I only know what I overheard my parents talking about."

"Which is…?"

"A bombing."

"What?!" I lunge to my feet and begin pacing again. "What bombing? Was he hurt? Why is it a secret? Is that why he's home? Did he lose—"

"T, slow down." Isabelle stands, grabs my arms, and pulls me toward her so she can wrap her arm around my shoulder.

"All I know is his unit was on a mission and there was a bombing. As far as I know, he wasn't physically hurt."

"Holy shit." The words leave my mouth in a rush. A flash of Isaiah punching the wall crashes into my brain. "Well, that makes a bit more sense."

"What does?"

"When we were arguing, his entire mood just, I don't know, shifted?" That's the only way I can think of to describe it to her. "He punched a hole in his bedroom wall, bled a bit."

"Seriously? He punched a hole in the wall with you right there?" Incredulity infuses her tone. "That's not like him at all."

"Think about it, Iz," I prompt. "It's the first thing that's made sense all day. If he has PTSD, he's gonna act differently, respond differently. I can't believe PTSD didn't even cross my mind as a possibility." I laugh without humor. "With what we do, what we've seen in our lives. Fuck, we're idiots."

"Why wouldn't he have talked to me about it? I mean, I'm his twin. I'm blood. Why?"

I lean my head against Isabelle's as silent tears stream down her cheeks. "Because he's in pain. And knowing Isaiah, he didn't want you to feel even a second's worth of worry. He may be going through some shit, but he loves you, Iz. He's always protected you and he always will."

Isabelle sniffles and stands up straight, grabbing my biceps in the process and turning me to face her.

"He loves you too, ya know?" She quirks a brow. "And I'm pretty sure he always will."

~

Beep... beep... beep...

I roll over and let out a groan at the sound of my alarm. I've never been a morning person, but after the events of yesterday, my brain is utterly exhausted. I stab my finger at the 'snooze' icon on my cell and pull the covers over my head to block out the light.

Nine minutes later, the beeping starts again. I toss the comforter off my body, sit up and rub my fists over my eyelids to clear my vision. A yawn escapes, and I stretch my arms above my head for a moment before turning the alarm off. I've got two hours to get my ass ready for the day and head to the shelter to pick up my client, Carla.

I stumble to the bathroom and turn on the shower to warm up while I undress. Tossing my clothes on the floor, I catch a glimpse of myself in the mirror and my eyes drop to the scars on my thighs. Nine slash marks. Eight of them are white and puckered, healed, while the last one, the one on the bottom left thigh, is a few day's old scab.

Turning away from my reflection, from the reminders of my weakness, I step into the shower to let the hot spray beat down on my body. I silently plead with the water to wash away my demons, the same as every other day. I resign myself to the fact that my demons aren't going anywhere and scrub my skin and hair as clean as I can.

After I dry and straighten my naturally curly locks, I get dressed in my favorite suit and head downstairs to the kitchen to get some coffee. As I let the caffeine do its job, I scroll through the news app on my phone and then check my email. Before I know it, it's time to leave.

Bag slung over my shoulder, I snatch my keys off the table by the front door. I unlock the deadbolt, open the barrier to the outside world, and come face to face with the one person I can't deal with right now.

"Mornin'."

Isaiah thrusts a travel mug at me and, without thinking, I take it. The grin on his face is encased in black stubble which tells me he didn't shave before leaving the house. It's also as fake as the knockoff Manolo Blahnik shoes I'm wearing and makes me think that he's trying his best to ignore what happened last night.

"Why are you here?" I ask with a bite to my tone.

"Because I was asked to be and because, as President, it's my job." He smirks. "Or at least, part of it." He shrugs as if things aren't awkward between us. "Figured it would be easier if we rode together."

A quick glance over his shoulder tells me he didn't think this through. "I can't ride Nyx to court."

"Why not?" The genuine confusion in his voice is comical. Seriously, he's not that stupid.

"Well, for starters, I'm dressed in a suit." I wave my hand in front of me to prove the point. "And second, I have to pick my client up. Where would she sit?"

"So, it's not because you're afraid to be close to me?"

"Of course not," I scoff, a little too quickly.

"Whatever you say, Til." Isaiah looks over his shoulder toward my own Harley parked in front of the garage. "What were you planning on driving?"

"Not that it's any of your business, but my car."

I flatten my free hand against his chest and push him backward so I can close and lock my door. Once that's done, I step around him and make my way to the garage. When I'm close, the motion sensor is tripped and the door slides open. Just one of the conveniences I had installed.

I pull open the driver's door of my gloss black BMW. Isaiah whistles behind me, startling me enough that I drop the travel mug and it clangs against the cement floor of the structure. I whirl around and glare at him.

"I suggest you move, otherwise you're gonna get hit when I back up."

Without waiting for a response, I climb in the vehicle and toss my bag on the passenger seat. I fire up the engine and check my rearview mirror to make sure Isaiah moved. Despite the warning, I wouldn't actually run him over. I don't think.

Isaiah isn't visible, and I let out a sigh of relief. I put the car in reverse, and just as I'm letting my foot up off the brake pedal, the passenger door flies open, and Isaiah sticks his head in.

"I'm coming with you," he announces as he moves my bag to the floor and climbs in next to me.

A quick glance at the clock on the dash tells me I now have no more time to argue so I say nothing. Once he shuts his door, I back out of the garage and point the BMW in the direction of the property gates. Dust billows behind us, and I force myself to slow down.

After five miles of complete silence, I turn on the stereo and crank up the volume. Scars by Papa Roach blares through the speakers, and I let the lyrics wash over me. Somehow, I forget that I have my iPhone set up to automatically sync when I'm in the car and it doesn't register that the song is from a playlist I created years ago. A playlist that I never intended for Isaiah to hear. When the song is over, I hit the 'back' button to play it again, out of habit.

"You missed me," Isaiah says from the passenger seat. There's no accusation in his tone, just awe, and acceptance.

I stab the power button and cut the music. "Fuck you, asshole," I snap. Immediately, what Isabelle told me last night hits me and I regret the words. I take a deep breath. "Sorry," I mumble.

"Come again?"

I spare him a glance and grasp the steering wheel tighter, my knuckles whiting with the force of my grip. "You heard me."

"I did. But that's definitely not a word I'm used to hearing from you."

"And you're not likely to hear it again so soak it up while you can."

"Better pay attention to the road or you'll miss your turn."

Isaiah turns his head to look out the window, effectively cutting off the conversation. Asshole. I know where I'm going.

Suffering through the silence, I head toward the shelter. Just before reaching the town limits, I turn left and weave my way down the winding gravel road, only stopping when I reach what most think is simply an industrial building. When I pull up in front of it, I turn the engine off and step out of the car. I don't bother to wait and see if Isaiah is following. It doesn't matter.

"We're picking your client up at an abandoned warehouse?"

I can see how he would think that. Hell, that's what people are supposed to think. Makes it harder for abusers to find. No name, no numbers, no identifying marks of any kind on the building.

I don't respond to him and simply walk around the side of the building, following the cracked cement path to the employee entrance. Isaiah is behind me the entire time, so close I can smell him. I punch in the code on the alarm box and wait for the tell-tale click of the lock disengaging.

Pulling open the door, I step aside and motion for him to go ahead of me. He folds his arms over his chest and stands there with his feet braced apart, his brow arched. I huff out a breath and stomp through the doorway. With my back to him, I stop fighting the slight tug of my lips into a grin.

Some things don't change.

"Care to tell me where we—"

"Tillie, you made it."

Carla, my client, wraps her arms around my neck and holds on tighter than necessary. I envelop her in a hug and let her hold on. Maybe some would say I'm crossing boundaries, but my clients have been through hell and back and I promised myself I wouldn't be the cold, calculating attorney that the courtroom demands of me. Not outside of the courthouse walls. And certainly not in their own home.

"I told you I'd be here," I remind her when I step back. Taking in the sleek black pantsuit I helped her pick from the shelter closet, I smile. "You look great."

"Thanks. It's not too mu—"

"It's not too anything, ma'am," Isaiah remarks from behind me.

Carla's hand flies to her chest as if she's just now realizing he's there. Her eyes grow round, and she instinctively lowers her gaze to the floor and takes a step back.

I glance at Isaiah over my shoulder and see the surprise on his face. It shouldn't be there. He's used to working with victims—no, survivors—of domestic violence. He was always good with them when we were younger.

He's been gone a long time, Til.

I reach out and grab Carla's hand, if for no other reason than to help ground her, provide her some comfort. "Carla, this is my…" I clear my throat. "This is Isaiah. We grew up together. He's going with us to the courthouse for the hearing. Added protection in case Brian pulls any shit."

"Nice to meet you, ma'am." Isaiah says softly, but with confidence. He doesn't extend his hand, seeming to have finally remembered some things he was taught, like no sudden movements.

Carla nods but doesn't make eye contact with Isaiah. She's made progress over the last year. I've been working with her, but she still has a long way to go.

I glance at the silver watch on my wrist to double-check the time. "We better get moving if we're going to get there before the jail transports Brian. We want to arrive before him."

"Smart," Isaiah remarks.

"I know." I glare at him.

He holds his hands up in surrender, but the grin on his face tells me he knows how much he's getting to me. And he's doing it on purpose.

I shake off my bad mood and lead Carla to my car. I fight the laugh that's threatening as Isaiah squeezes his large frame into the backseat so Carla can sit upfront with me. Carla isn't as able to hide her reaction, and for the first time since she noticed Isaiah standing behind me, she smiles.

And that smile, that one moment of genuine happiness, is why I do what I do and take on the fights of others.

7

ISAIAH

"Is this who you're fucking now?"

I step between the man raising his voice and a very tense Carla. So, this must be Brian. I quickly scan the room and make note of the sheriff talking to someone across the aisle and Tillie in deep conversation with Henry.

"Answer me you stupid—"

I flatten my hand on his chest, stepping in when clearly no one else is. "Listen here, *Brian.* Who Carla sleeps with is none of your business anymore. You lost the right to have a say in that the second you chose to rape your wife." I straighten the shirt the public defender must have brought for him based on its large size and pat his chest. "Now, go sit down next to your lawyer."

Brian seems to recognize that his outburst was the wrong tactic and he switches gears. He tries to step around me, but I stop him, forcing him to lean to the side so he can look at his wife. "Carla, baby, c'mon," he pleads. "You know I didn't mean to do it. I was drunk and you know what alcohol does to me. Please, baby—"

"Brian, stop!" Carla shouts from behind me and all eyes in

the courtroom turn to us. "Just stop it. I've taken you back so many times. I'm done." She takes a deep breath and sighs. "I don't love you anymore."

With those parting words, she takes a seat behind the prosecution's side of the courtroom. Tillie immediately excuses herself from her conversation with Henry and joins her client. I make my way to Carla's other side so that we flank her.

I lean over and whisper, "You did good."

Carla gives me a small smile before tucking her hair behind her ears. When she does that, I notice a scar next to her eye for the first time. *Motherfucker!* I hope like hell Brian gets what's coming to him in prison. I catch sight of Tillie and see her mouth 'thank you' and I simply nod.

Over the next few minutes, there's a flurry of activity and then the judge enters, and the bailiff instructs us all to rise. Opening statements are given and as much as I should be paying attention, all I can focus on is Tillie's bouncing leg. Not only is it shaking the bench, but my eyes are drawn to her ankles just below the hem of her pants and above the leather of her heels.

Her smooth, tanned skin draws me in, and I imagine my hands wrapping around her calf, slowly caressing her flesh as I work my way up her thigh, paying special attention to the spot that I know drives her crazy.

"Isaiah!"

I whip my head up and see Tillie and Carla staring at me like they're waiting for something.

"Huh?"

"Carla's been called to testify. You need to let her out." Tillie narrows her eyes at me as if trying to figure out what was consuming my attention. "Now."

"Right."

I shift so that Carla can make her way to the witness

stand. Her body is tense, and she doesn't look toward the defendant. As she answers the questions presented to her, I dip my head and look at Tillie out of the corner of my eye. Her leg is no longer bouncing but her fingers are curled around the edge of the bench. And if I'm not mistaken, she's a few inches closer to me.

I make a point to listen to the testimony and watch Tillie's reactions. The longer Carla is on the witness stand, the closer Tillie gets to me. *Interesting.*

"No further questions." Henry sits down, adjusts his tie, and then over his shoulder, he winks at Tillie.

The defense cross-examines Carla and she holds up well under the smarmy bastard's accusations. She seems like a smart woman and knows that what happened to her isn't her fault, nor is alcohol consumption to blame.

"You may step down," the judge instructs when all questions are asked.

Brian's gaze tracks Carla's every movement. Even from across the room, I can see the rage in his eyes, the intense evil that lies within him. And I should be able to recognize it. I've seen enough of it throughout my life, both in and out of the military.

The remainder of the trial goes fairly quickly. There are a few character witnesses for good ol' Brian but the jury doesn't seem to be moved by their testimony. When the judge hands the case over to the jury and the sheriff steps up to get Brian and return him to the jail, all hell breaks loose.

With lightning-quick speed, Brian evades the handcuffs and makes a grab for the sheriff's weapon. He wraps his fingers around the butt of the gun and waves it around maniacally. The public defender jumps out of the way and I instinctively grab Carla and Tillie and shove them behind me.

The sound of the gavel banging against the judge's bench,

along with shouts, grunts, and groans as the sheriff, Liam, and the other Brotherhood members tackle Brian to the floor fill the air. White-hot rage rolls through me, from my head to my toes. Brian is lucky it was everyone else who got their hands on him because if it were me, I'd kill him. Not only for being a complete dumbass but for putting Tillie's life in danger.

I'm able to keep my visceral response in check but only because of the two small hands twisting in the back of my shirt. They aren't Tillie's hands. And the fact that I can tell that without looking only makes my blood simmer more.

"I'm getting you both out of here," I say to the two women.

I reach back and grab Carla's hand. I try to grab Tillie's as well, but she dodges me. Guiding Carla out of the room, we make our way outside and once the fresh air hits my skin, I feel a cold calm overtake me. I stand with Carla on the courthouse steps and make a point to look her over for any signs that she's not okay.

"That was..." Carla shakes her head.

"Scary, I know." I grip her shoulders. "But you're safe, I promise. After that stunt, the bastard's not going anywhere any time soon."

"That's great, but not what I was gonna say." I arch a questioning brow. "That was awesome," she clarifies, causing me to chuckle. "Watching Brian get what was coming to him... that was great."

The smile that tugs her lips upward is beaming and I love it. This is why I've done what I've done. To help people. To see them walk through the fire and come out the other side a happier, better version of themselves. Sure, the fire may cause burns, scars, permanent reminders, but it all disappears under their newfound selves.

Carla and I wait for another twenty-three minutes—not

that I'm keeping track—and finally, the door opens and Liam steps through, with the others at his back. I search for Tillie and when I don't see her, my shoulders deflate involuntarily.

"Glad you were here." Liam steps up to me and rests his hand on my shoulder. "It's good to have you home."

"I'm glad I was too," I respond, but my focus is not on him. I keep shifting my gaze to the door, watching for *her*.

Aiden steps up next to Liam. "She said to go ahead and take Carla back to the shelter." He tosses me Tillie's car keys and I catch them easily. "Remember how to get there?"

"Uh, yeah."

"Henry will bring her home later."

"Right," I mumble. "Henry."

"I'm gonna give you a bit of unsolicited advice, son," Aiden starts. "Figure your own shit out before you go after my baby girl."

"Yes, si—"

"I'm not done." Aiden glances at Liam who seems to take the hint and guides Carla toward the car. When it's just the two of us, he continues. "I've been where you are. Shit, we all have. I know what it's like coming back from war, what it's like when it's not necessarily your decision. I also know what it's like to have your head so twisted up that you don't know which way is up or down. I know you love my daughter." He chuckles. "Fuck, you always have. But fix you first. Because if you hurt her, if you fuck with her again and then decide that you need to walk away, I will hunt you down and make you suffer. Understood?"

"Yes, sir." I give a curt nod.

My guts are in a knot, my heart is hammering against my ribs. Visions of military raids, dead bodies, bombs exploding all collide with flashes of Tillie laughing and carefree, Tillie standing there when I said 'goodbye', and Tillie crying behind a door after I crushed her.

Maybe Aiden is right. Maybe I do need to fix myself first. Problem with that is, I'm afraid the only thing that can fix me, the only thing that will make me feel whole again is the one thing I have no business wanting.

Tillie.

8

TILLIE

Eight years ago...

"I'm going with you."

Arms crossed over my chest, I stare at Micah and my father. Isaiah graduates from basic training tomorrow and there is no way I'm going to miss it. I don't give a flying fuck what anyone says.

My dad and Micah share a look and my heart drops. "What?" I demand. "Spit it out. I'm a big girl, I can take it." I'm not so sure I can but they don't have to know that.

"Peanut," my dad starts. "There's just not enough tickets for all of us to go to the ceremony."

"Bullshit," I counter. "Isaiah will make sure there's one for me."

Micah sighs. "And if he can't?"

"Then I'll wait at the hotel and see him after." My inner child comes out and I pout. "I want to see him. It's been eight weeks. And I know he'll want to see me."

Again, that look. That look that screams at me that I'm wrong, that they know something I don't.

You're overreacting, Til. Isaiah misses you. He's just been too busy to write or call. It's fine. Everything is fine.

"So, what time do we leave?" I ask, not giving them any more room to argue.

"Sadie and I are heading out in a few hours," Micah responds. "If it's okay with your dad, you can ride with us."

I glance at my dad and raise a brow. "Fine. But Peanut, don't get your hopes up, okay?"

I nod but don't comment. I also make no effort to walk away. I stare at two of the most important men in my life. Sometimes, in moments like these, I feel older than my eighteen years. I recognize how life has taken a toll on them. They both have gray hair and if asked, will say it's because of us kids. There are more wrinkles on their faces. Some are from laughter, some from the sun, but mostly it's from the work that we do, that they do.

I launch myself at my dad, suddenly feeling like I have to hold on to him, never let him go. His arms come around me and he lifts me off the ground. My worries about Isaiah, about Micah and my dad hiding something from me, melt away and I rest my head on his shoulder.

"I love you, daddy."

"Love you, too, Peanut." He sets me on my feet and turns toward Micah. "You'll tell Isaiah that Scarlett and I are damn proud of him?"

"Of course."

"Thanks." Dad shakes Micah's hand and then returns his attention to me. "I'm gonna go pick your sister up from school. Be careful, okay."

"Always."

"We'll keep an eye on her. Don't worry."

Dad nods and then walks away. Micah shifts toward me and smiles.

"What?" I ask when he says nothing.

"Did you know that I was there the night your dad found out about you?"

"Yeah, yeah," I joke because I've heard this story a million times. "Mom showed up at the hospital. I was with her and dad was called. He fell in love with me the second he saw me, and I've had him wrapped around my finger ever since."

"Okay, smartass." Micah chuckles. "Come sit down for a minute. I want to tell you a part of that story that you might not know."

I follow him to the couch and sit down, fighting back the memories of Isaiah and me on the couch, watching movies, making out, talking. It dips under Micah's weight as he settles next to me and slings an arm around my shoulders.

"So, your dad calls me in the middle of the night, right?" I nod to let him know I'm listening. "Doesn't tell me anything other than he needs me at the hospital and to 'bring a damn car seat'. That's it. No details, nothing. Of course, I do exactly that because I'd never heard him so… out of his depth."

"Really?" I have a hard time believing that. "He's always so in control."

"Not that night." He squeezes my shoulder. "When I got to the hospital, he was a wreck. Convinced himself that I was going to be angry with him for having a relationship with your mom."

"Why?"

The idea that Micah could ever be mad about my mom or me is ludicrous. He's been nothing but kind and loving, to everyone that's a part of the club.

"Because, you don't sleep with clients," Micah responds, not sugarcoating anything. "Your mom was a client before she was, well, your mom."

"I knew that, but I never knew that it was against the rules or anything."

"It was." Micah shrugs. "But it was an unspoken rule and even though your dad was the funny man of the group, he also did not bend the rules. Until Scarlett."

"I can see that. He's always giving me a hard time about rules and stuff. I mean, I'm eighteen years old. I'm an adult. And he still treats me like a kid."

"Honey, you're always going to be his little girl. Always." He pats my knee. "And that's why I'm telling you all of this. That night, your dad took one look at you, with your blonde curls and blue eyes and an attitude to boot, and that was it. He loved you. He'd never stopped loving your mom so that wasn't an issue. But you were wary of men." I scoff because I remember. I remember feeling afraid and dad being patient. I remember how he did everything he could to show me he loved me.

"I remember," I mumble, not wanting to, not now.

"He vowed, from that moment on, that you would always be safe, loved, protected, and that he wouldn't let anyone hurt you ever again."

"He can't stop life from happening," I say.

"No, but he can try. And one of the things he wants to protect you from is my son." Micah holds his hand up to silence me when I open my mouth to protest. "Hold on a sec, honey. I love my son. He and Isabelle and Sadie… they're my world, along with the club family, but your dad's not wrong."

I stand up so fast that my head spins. "He is wrong! Isaiah would never hurt me!"

Micah rises and stands in front of me to stop me from pacing. "Tillie, open your eyes, honey." He grips my shoulders. "Has Isaiah called?" I shake my head. "Has he written you at all?" Again, I shake my head. "I know he loves you and I know you love him, but you're both still young." Micah spots the tears falling from my eyes and wipes them away with a thumb. "All I'm saying is maybe this is a good time for you to figure out who you are without him. And it's a good time for him to work through whatever the hell is in his head that makes him think he doesn't belong in the club, that his place isn't as president someday."

Silent tears continue to fall and Micah pulls me to him, comforting me as he always has when he dishes out his tough love. He's right about my dad. He tries to protect me and that extends to him spoiling me. It's usually my mom or Micah who dole out the harsher life lessons. When I finally calm down, I step away from him and glare.

"I'm still going," I say with conviction.

Micah's grin returns. "I figured."

~

"You're man enough to join the military, go to BUD/S training, serve your damn country, so don't be a chicken shit when it comes to that girl in there."

Micah's voice booms through the hotel room door as he yells at Isaiah. I can hear footsteps as one, or both, of them, paces in front of my room, and the only thing that registers, other than Micah's rage, is the words BUD/S training. *Navy Seals?*

"Pops, I can't do it." Isaiah's voice isn't as confident as I'm used to and that only makes what I'm hearing worse. "You know it's going to break her heart."

Too late.

"Get your ass in that room and talk to her," Micah demands.

"Isaiah," Sadie cuts in, her voice softer but no less harsh and angry. "You two have been inseparable since the moment Aiden brought her home. You owe her an explanation. Especially after you told her you'd be together after eight weeks."

"I can't," Isaiah repeats with a bite to his tone.

"Why not? I didn't raise a coward."

"Because," Isaiah snaps. "Because she's..."

"She's what?" Sadie asks when Isaiah doesn't finish.

"Because she's the only one who can talk me out of this!"

I rear back from the door as if burned by his words. The confidence that I know so well, that I've always loved, is back. But he's not the same Isaiah. He's not the boy I fell in love with when I was ten years old. He's a man. And he's making a decision that is tearing me apart from the inside out. But he's right. I will try to talk him out of it. And because he's right, I know what I have to do. Time to woman up.

I take a deep breath and reach for the doorknob. It takes several false starts, but I manage to yank it open and when I do, all eyes turn to me. I don't look at Micah or Sadie. No, all of my focus is on the sculpted body of the man who, in the space of a few minutes, has gutted me.

"Can Isaiah and I get a minute, please?" I ask without taking my eyes off of his.

"Honey, maybe you should go back—"

"Please," I snap.

"Sure," Micah responds. I still don't look at them, but I see him wrap his arms around Sadie's shoulders out of the corner of my eye. "C'mon, Sweetness. Let's give them a few minutes. And Tillie?"

"Yes?"

"We're just down the hall if you need anything, okay?"

I allow a small smile and finally cut my eyes to Micah. "Thanks. I'll be fine."

As soon as they walk past Isaiah and down the hall, I refocus on his features. He's filled out, *a lot,* in the last eight weeks. He looks good... too damn good. My fingers itch to touch him so I shove my hands in my pockets.

"Tillie, I'm—"

"Don't," I murmur, cutting him off. "Don't talk. Just listen."

He rocks back on his feet and nods. "Okay."

"I'm not going to stop you from going to BUD/S. If that's what you want to do, then I support that decision."

"You do?"

He sounds genuinely confused and I suppose he would be. I didn't know this is what was going to happen until I reached for the doorknob.

"Let me finish." I let my head fall back and I stare at the ceiling for a minute to gather my thoughts. When I finally look at him, I'm as sure of my decision as I'm ever going to be, so I don't mince words. "I will support you because you're my best friend and that's what friends do, no matter how much it hurts. I will support you because I fucking love you and that's what I'm supposed to do. But know this… I'm not going to sit around and wait for you to get your head out of your ass. I can't be the person you call or write when you're missing home. I can't be the person you think of to get you through the hell of it all. And I can't be the woman who sits at home waiting for her man to return. I can't. And I won't."

I lock eyes with him and swallow past the lump in my throat.

You got this far, Til. Only two more words.

"Goodbye, Isaiah."

And with that, I kiss his cheek and turn away to return to my room. The door quietly clicks as I shut it, careful not to let it slam. I stand there, staring at the closed curtains across the room, waiting until I hear some sign that Isaiah has walked away. For a few seconds, it's silent. But then I hear something that makes me crumble.

A thump on the door sounds, not loud, but as if he's leaned his forehead against the barrier.

"I love you, Tillie." A heaving sigh. "Thank you."

That moment, the moment he thanks me for lying through my teeth to make him feel better guts me. I crumble to the floor and let the tears fall, unchecked.

Now what?

9

ISAIAH

Present Day...

"Another?"

I nod at the bartender and slide my empty bottle across the wooden bar top. She tosses it in the trash, and I'm jolted by the clinking sound it makes against the rest of the discarded glass. I watch as she reaches into the ice chest and pulls out an ice-cold bottle of Deadeye Stout, a local brew I missed while I was gone.

"You new around here?" she asks when she sets the bottle on a coaster in front of me.

"Are you?" I grumble in response.

I lift the beer to my lips and take a long pull, never taking my eyes off of her while I do.

"Hardly," she huffs. "Been here a few years. We get a lot of regulars in Dusty's but I've never seen you."

As she wipes down the bar with a rag, I contemplate my answer. The truth is, I may have grown up here, but I suppose I am new, depending on how you look at it.

"Grew up here," I finally settle on. "But I've been gone a while."

She stares at me as if waiting to see if I'm going to elaborate. I'm not. She gives a tight smile and steps back, tossing the rag in the sink behind the bar.

"Got it. Not a talker."

She walks toward the other end of the long counter and takes the orders of two guys that just came in. The sway of her hips catches my attention, along with her perfectly rounded ass. I already noticed the way her cleavage spilled over the lace front of her top and mentally debated on whether or not to hit on her. Maybe I should rethink my decision.

I twist on the barstool and face the crowd of customers. There's a healthy mix of men and women, all of whom appear to be having a good time dancing, drinking, laughing. I'm the exception to the rule though.

I came to Dusty's because drinking myself stupid seemed like a better idea than sitting at home listening for the sound of a car engine that would tell me that Tillie was home. I haven't seen her since the scene at the courthouse and the thought of her spending the rest of her day with Henry gnaws at my mind.

The bartender returns and leans against the liquor shelves behind her. We lock eyes and, if I'm not mistaken, she'd take me up on anything I have to offer if I choose to do so.

She nods toward the customers she just served. "They tell me you're connected to the Broken Rebel Brotherhood."

"I am," I confirm, feeling a sense of pride.

"Great people. Helped me through a rough patch." When I make no comment, she asks, "Do you know Sadie, the president's wife?"

I smile at the thought of my mother and don't bother to correct her about the president thing. "I do."

"She's incredible. To use what she went through with her first husband to help other women… I admire her."

At the reminder of the abuse, my mother suffered at the hands of her ex-husband, Ian, my muscles coil and my grip on the beer bottle tightens. The fucker not only beat the shit out of her, but he also pretended to be someone else and dated Brie. It was a clusterfuck. Fortunately, my dad stepped in and everything ended well, but it could have gone a completely different way.

I listen with half an ear as she goes on about how great the club is, how they all helped her turn her life around. I want to care, to be proud of what the club did, but all I feel is an overwhelming sense of jealousy and self-doubt.

"I can see I'm boring you."

She pushes off the ledge of the counter behind her and reaches to grab my now empty bottle. I quickly snake my arm out and wrap my fingers around her wrist. Not too tight, but enough to pull her up short.

"I'm sorry," I say, giving her an apologetic look. "Been a rough day. Shit, it's been a rough few years."

She turns her hand in my grasp and holds onto my wrist. "Don't worry about it. You obviously came in here to be alone and I'm babbling like an idiot."

"No, you're not. I did come in here to be alone, but I should've known that wouldn't happen in a bar." I chuckle at myself in a self-deprecating manner. "You mentioned Sadie and it threw me off a bit. Took me to a place I didn't want to go." She tilts her head in question. "Sadie is my mom."

"Holy shit!" She yanks her hand back and covers her mouth for a brief moment. When she drops her arms to her sides, her face softens. "I'm sorry. I had no idea."

"Of course, you didn't."

"God, I feel like such an idiot."

"Don't. Really, it's fine." I lean my elbows on the bar. "Listen, why don't we start over? Would that help?"

"Yes," she rushes to say. "Yeah, that'd be great."

I laugh at her but not in a mocking way. She's gorgeous and I can tell she genuinely feels bad. I reach out a hand to shake hers.

"Hi. I'm Isaiah," I introduce myself. "The new president of the Broken Rebel Brotherhood. And you are?"

She takes my offered hand. "Ruby. Dusty's niece."

"Nice to meet you, Ruby." I break contact with her. "I didn't realize that Dusty had a niece. How long have you worked here?"

"A few years." Her smile is sad. "I inherited the bar when my uncle passed. How long have you been gone?"

"Sorry for your loss." I didn't know that Dusty had died and the news is like a sucker punch to the gut. One more person lost to the world. "I, uh, I've been gone a few years."

"Fair enough."

"So, Ruby… what time do you get off tonight?"

"I'm here till close so…"

I pull out my phone to check the time. I got to Dusty's around ten and I'm shocked to see that it's already after midnight. I miss the rest of what Ruby is saying as I also note the amount of missed calls from my dad. There are text messages from Izzy, Aiden, Brie, and my mom, as well.

"I, uh, I'm sorry, Ruby. I gotta go."

I don't wait for her response and based on the dramatic huff I hear behind me, she's pissed. Unfortunately for her, I don't give a damn. Sure, I thought that maybe the night could have ended with us sharing a bed but now that I'm home, family comes first.

I listen to the first voicemail as I walk outside.

"Isaiah, I need you to call me." My father's voice booms through the line and I can hear the stress in his voice. "Now."

I continue to walk toward my bike and scroll until I reach the last voicemail from my dad and hit play.

"Dammit, Isaiah. Get your head outta your ass and answer your goddamn phone."

I switch to the texting app and tap the screen to read through some of them. The more texts I read, the more urgent they become. When I reach Nyx, I pull my key out of my pocket and, just as I'm about to throw my leg over to straddle the seat, the sound of a roaring engine draws my attention to the road.

I watch as a familiar SUV pulls in and stops next to me. Liam climbs out of the driver's seat of the club Jeep and launches a fist at my face. Fortunately for me, I dodge the blow and manage to grab his clenched fist and wrestle his arm behind his back.

"What the fuck, Liam?"

"Maybe if you'd answer your phone I wouldn't have been dying to pummel you." He struggles against my hold and I shove him away from me. When he turns around, the scowl on his face says it all. There's more to his rage than my phone answering habits. "Are you sober enough to drive or am I gonna have to drive your drunk ass?"

"I'm sober enough," I snap. "Where are we going?"

I listen with half an ear as I look back to my phone to glance at the unread text messages. I catch a few of the words coming out of Liam's mouth: hospital, attack, not good. But it's the last text I read, from Isabelle, that has my blood boiling.

Tillie was attacked. Need you at the hospital.

"Jesus Christ," I mumble as I run a shaky hand through

my short hair. My mind reels with all of the possibilities and dozens of questions. I return my gaze to Liam and glare. "What the hell happened?"

"Do you really wanna stand here and go over the details?" He tracks my movements as I finally throw my leg over my bike. My hands are shaking, and my vision is hazy. "Fucking hell. Get in the damn Jeep. You can get your bike tomorrow."

I glare at him for a moment before allowing myself to do what I'm told. I'm not drunk, but my mind is reeling, and driving right now is probably a very bad idea.

"What do you know about what happened to Tillie?" I ask when the silence stretches on after we leave Dusty's parking lot.

"Not much," he admits. "She was out with her douchebag boyfriend and—"

"Henry attacked her?" I whirl in my seat to face Liam, rage threatening to tear out of me.

"What?" He glances at me for a second before returning his attention to the road. "No, he didn't attack her."

"But you said..." I think back over what he actually said.

"I called him a douchebag." He shrugs. "I don't like the guy."

"Why not? What's wrong with him?"

"Fuck, bro. You really don't see it, do you?" he asks incredulously.

"See what?"

"No one likes Henry!" he shouts. "Jesus. Even Tillie's feelings for him are questionable." He takes a deep breath and tightens his grip on the wheel, expertly weaving in and out of traffic as he navigates his way to the hospital. "He's not you."

"What's that supposed to mean?"

"It means, oh stupid one, that you and Tillie seem to be the only two people on the planet who haven't realized that you are meant to be together."

Liam's words slam into me so forcefully that I fall back against the passenger door, reeling from the implications. As much as I want to ask questions, I force my focus back to the current situation.

"Finish telling me what happened," I demand in a steely quiet tone.

Liam heaves a sigh. "Tillie and Henry were out, and he was going to drive her home, but she insisted that she'd be fine and she'd find her own way."

"Stubborn woman."

"Yeah, too stubborn for her own good." Liam stops at a red light and a quick glance around tells me we're a few blocks from the hospital. "Anyway, she called for an Uber. I talked to the staff at the restaurant and they say she waited inside and when the Uber arrived, she left. Said nothing seemed off."

"Okay…" I draw the word out, not sure where this is going other than she's now in the fucking hospital.

"The Uber driver is the one who attacked her."

"So, they caught the guy?"

"Not exactly."

"What the fuck is that supposed to mean?"

"A passerby saw her lying on the side of the road and called 911. She was transported to the hospital. She's given as much information as she can to the cops and they're working on tracking him down. They're not getting far because apparently, the Uber driver didn't actually work for Uber and his name and info was fake."

"We'll find him." Determination laces my tone.

"We will. Shit, my dad can find anyone."

His reference to his dad is reassuring. Griffin has always been the club member that can track anyone down online. He's the resident guru on that kinda stuff. The original members may have taken a step back but for one of our own, for Tillie, it'll be all hands on deck.

Liam pulls into the parking lot of the ER department at the hospital and I don't even wait for the Jeep to come to a stop before I'm throwing open the door and racing for the entrance. I hear Liam call out to me to wait for him, but I ignore his pleas.

I seek out the other BRB members in the waiting room and zero in on my dad. I stride toward him and my hackles raise when I see the censure in his expression, the disappointment.

"Where the fuck have you been? You're the president now and people need to be able to get a hold of you." He growls when I step in front of him.

"How is she?" I ask, ignoring his question.

"Physically, she'll be okay." He runs a weathered hand over his face and through his beard. "Emotionally, she's got a long road ahead of her."

"I wanna see her," I demand, looking around the room as if she'll step out from behind a curtain at any moment.

Dad nods toward a flimsy blue curtain behind me. "She's over there. Henry is in—"

I miss the rest of what he says because I walk away and straight toward Tillie. Voices register from behind the curtain, but I don't care. I yank the blue material aside and see Tillie, bruised and battered on the bed, and Henry standing next to her. I have to swallow back the bile that threatens at the back of my throat. Two trips to the ER in two days. Definitely not the way I wanted to be welcomed home.

My gaze goes straight to her hand. Henry is trying to hold it, but she keeps pulling away.

"What are you doing here?" Henry asks, staring daggers at me.

Ignoring his question, I step to the other side of the bed and pick up Tillie's hand. It isn't lost on me, or Henry based on his narrowed eyes, that she doesn't pull away. Henry bristles and the air in the room becomes thick with tension.

"I asked you a question."

I shift my attention to Henry and arch a brow. "I heard you."

"Then answer me," he grates out from between clenched teeth.

"I don't owe you an answer."

"Yes, you do. Tillie is no longer your con—"

"I asked them to call Isaiah."

10

TILLIE

Isaiah's eyes widen at my admission, as do Henry's. On Henry, the look is annoying but on Isaiah, it's just sad. I allow my own eyes to slide closed as pain radiates through my body and threatens to explode from the top of my head.

"Tillie, why would—"

"Not now, Henry."

I roll my neck and open my eyes to look at him. He's angry and I can't help the involuntary shudder that rolls through me at the sight of him. Isaiah's large fingers gently squeeze my hand from the other side of me and I squeeze back.

"Look, I'm tired and hurt like hell," I start, never taking my eyes off of Henry. "Can we maybe talk tomorrow?"

"What about him?" Henry nods toward Isaiah with a scowl.

"I'll leave if she asks me to, but I haven't heard her ask me yet," Isaiah says.

I roll my eyes at the challenge in his tone but try to smile through the pain at Henry. "It's fine, I promise." Henry doesn't look convinced. "The doc said they aren't holding me. I'll be discharged soon and I'm gonna sleep like the dead tonight. I'll call you first thing in the morning."

Henry's eyes dart back and forth between me and Isaiah several times before his facial expression softens. "Fine, I'll go. I'll grab some things from my place and meet you at yours."

"No, Henry." I shake my head and instantly regret it when the throbbing increases. "Just go home. *Please.*"

Henry still makes no move to leave. Isaiah, his frustration matching my own, drops my hand and makes his way to the end of the bed where he stands with his feet braced apart and his arms folded over his chest.

"You're a smart man, Henry. Tillie asked you nicely to leave." Isaiah lowers his voice. "Now, how would it look if the prosecutor himself got thrown out of a hospital for harassment?"

I can't stop the snort that escapes and that only serves to piss off Henry more. I sober my expression and mock glare at Isaiah. All he does is shrug like he has no idea what's wrong.

Henry continues to stare at Isaiah, incredulously, but when Isaiah still doesn't back down, Henry settles and leans over to kiss my cheek. "I'll see you tomorrow," he whispers in my ear.

Henry straightens and strides toward where the curtain separates so he can leave, pausing and glancing over his shoulder at me. "I love you, Tillie."

He doesn't wait for a response before leaving and I'm glad because I don't think I could have brought myself to tell him the same in return. Not in front of Isaiah. Not when it's Isaiah, not Henry, I wanted the second I was dumped out of that car.

"Damn, I thought I was gonna have to pick him up and carry him outta here."

Isaiah's tone is light, but I know him well enough to know he's not joking. "Shut up, asshole," I say, no heat in my own tone.

He turns to face me and rests his hands on the rail at the end of the bed. "Really gonna need you to quit calling me that, Til."

"I'll quit calling you that when you stop being one."

Isaiah shakes his head and chuckles. Several tense moments pass before he makes his way to the side of the bed and sits in the ugly pink chair. He stretches his long legs out but then seems to think better of it and tucks them under the chair and leans over the bed to pick up my hand in his.

"Aw, Til, what happened?" He asks as he sweeps a strand of hair out of my face and behind my ear. I look away from him, but he softly grips my chin and forces my gaze back to his. "Til, baby, talk to me."

I search his eyes, for what, I don't know. What I find is more than I'm prepared for, more than I deserve.

"It was a normal night," I begin, after taking a deep breath and swallowing past my fear. "Henry took me out for dinner and drinks. Nothing special."

Isaiah maintains his hold on my hand and rubs his thumb over my knuckles. Back and forth, back and forth. His touch is soothing, calming.

"Henry wanted to go home, and I wanted to have a few more drinks." I glance at him out of the corner of my eye. "Been a rough few days, ya know?"

Isaiah chuckles without humor. "So, you thought drinking would help?"

"Where were you at tonight?" I counter.

"Touché."

"That's what I thought." I let my head fall back against the flat pillow. "I called for an Uber and when they arrived, everything seemed normal." Flashes of memory send shivers through my body, which only triggers pain. "I noticed too late that the driver wasn't going in the right direction. When I questioned him about it, he got angry."

I break out into a cold sweat as I recall what happened next. "He drove down a dirt road, one I didn't recognize. I tried to run when he got out, but I couldn't get the door open. I guess he had the child locks on or something."

Isaiah's grip tightens and a quick glance reveals his taut jaw and narrowed eyes. If he's angry now, he's gonna be livid in a minute.

"Uh," I drop my gaze to where he's grasping my hand. "You're hurting me."

"Shit."

Isaiah drops my hand and reels back. His eyes are on my face, shifting as he takes in my colorful bruises and the lacerations.

"What happened next?" he asks tremulously.

I swallow past the lump in my throat and fix my stare on the biohazard container on the wall just beyond Isaiah. "He, um, he yanked me out of the car, threw me to the ground." Swallow. "I'm pretty sure he had steel toe boots on. He kicked me and broke a few ribs." Swallow. "I fought as hard as I could." I lift my hands, which are covered in defensive wounds, to prove it. "Wasn't hard enough. He, uh, beat the hell outta me." Swallow. Deep breath. Swallow.

"Did he...?"

"No." I shake my head slightly and my bottom lip quivers. "He... he, um, tried." Tears spill over my lashes as I remember slender hands yanking my pants down my legs. "I guess he doesn't like a fight. He couldn't get it up." I try to inject humor into my voice, try to make this whole retelling somewhat less painful, but I fail miserably. "I think that's why he stopped. He was mad at himself." I finally return my eyes to Isaiah's. "He picked me up and tossed me in the backseat. He drove around for a bit and then, at some point, he pulled to the side of the road and demanded I get out. I basically rolled out of the car and must have passed out because the next thing I remember is waking up here."

Silence hangs in the air when I finish. I fidget with a loose string on the sheet that's covering me and roll it into a ball between my fingers. Isaiah rises from the chair and paces, mussing up his hair with his hands. Every few seconds, he drops the f-bomb and I know he's trying to work through all the information I gave him.

I track his movement and just as he faces me and opens his mouth to speak, the curtain is thrust to the side, and the doctor appears.

"Miss Winters, I'm going to be discharging you here shortly." He flips through the chart in his hand. "It says here you live alone." He glances at me. "I'm going to be sending you home with high dose pain medication. Is there someone that can stay with you for a few days?"

"I'll be staying with her," Isaiah booms from his position against the wall.

My head whips to his and dizziness washes over me. Once it subsides, I try to argue. "No, you won't be." I look at the doctor. "I've got a friend that will stay. I'm sure she's in the waiting room."

"Isabelle is in the waiting room but she's gonna be busy." Isaiah's tone says it's not open for discussion. Not wanting to fight in front of a stranger, I keep my mouth shut. "I'll be with her, doc. I'll make sure she doesn't do anything she's not supposed to."

"Good, good," the doctor says, oblivious to the tension in the room. "You're going to be sore for a few weeks. Take the meds as directed. I've listed a few therapists in your discharge papers that you may want to call. You've been through quite a trauma and I highly recommend you talk to someone."

I roll my eyes and catch Isaiah doing the same. Not that we don't believe in therapy. We'd be hypocrites if we didn't, considering what our family is involved in, but I'm not a talker about my feelings. Never have been and never will be.

The doctor reviews the discharge instructions with me while a nurse removes my IV. I'm glad Isaiah is here because my brain is a bit fuzzy from the pain medicine I was already given. When the doctor leaves us alone again, Isaiah folds the discharge papers and shoves them in his back pocket before stepping up to the bed.

"C'mon, Til, let me help you get dressed." Isaiah reaches for my hand and I flinch. Hurt flashes in his eyes, but he doesn't retreat. Instead, he latches on to my hand, gently, and puts an arm under my back to ease me up. "I'll make it quick and... well, I'll make it quick."

I smirk at him and he shrugs sheepishly. I allow him to help me up but when he tries to lift the sheet, I groan, and he stops. He seems to get that I'm not okay with baring all to him. What he doesn't know is I have scars I don't want him to see either. It takes some maneuvering, but he manages to get me dressed with minimal exposure.

I lean against him for support and just as we're about to clear the damn blue curtain, I tip my head back and dig in my heels.

"What is it, Til?" Isaiah asks.

"I just..." I try to gather my thoughts and then spit out two of the hardest words for me to say to him. "Thank you."

11

ISAIAH

Sunlight streams through the curtains in Tillie's bedroom, casting shadows along the walls while simultaneously illuminating her sleeping form under the blankets. I watch as she tosses and turns, mumbling in her sleep as if caught in a nightmare. I push myself off of the doorframe and stride toward her, only to stop when a knock on the door catches my attention.

I retrace my steps to see who's knocking and can't help but be shocked by how *normal* Tillie's house looks. I always pictured her surrounding herself with all things Harley Davidson. The vision in my mind leaned more toward badass biker chick, not a sophisticated woman.

Henry stares back at me through the glass of the front door. I cross my arms over my chest and glare, tempted to leave him out in the cool morning air. Remembering that he's someone that Tillie supposedly gives a damn about, I drop my arms and open the door.

"What the hell are you doing here?" Henry demands as he pushes past me and glances around the living room. "Where's Tillie?"

Don't do it, Isaiah. Don't do—

"She's still in bed." And I did it. "It was a long night." To add insult to injury, I wink.

Henry bristles and his face turns red. He whirls around and takes the steps two at a time. I lunge after him and manage to grab his arm to stop him before he charges into Tillie's room.

"Jesus, dude." I force him to face me. I drag him back downstairs, him resisting with what I assume is all of his pitiful strength. "It was a joke." As much as goading him seems fun, Tillie won't appreciate it, and I don't want his jealous ass waking her up. "She *is* still sleeping though. I'm sure you can imagine how tired she is after what she went through last night."

Henry's gaze focuses on the stairs, no doubt picturing her sleeping soundly in her bed. "Right. Of course." He returns his attention to me. "Sorry."

"No, you're not." I shrug to let him know I don't really give a damn.

"You still haven't answered me," Henry complains.

"I know."

"I'm Tillie's boyfriend. I think I have a right to know." Henry runs his hands over the lapels of his suit jacket.

"Look, Til and I go way back." I lean against the back of the couch and cross one ankle over the other. "I'm always going to be around so you might as well get used to it."

"Like you were around the last eight years?" Henry taunts. His lips tilt into a grin at my obvious frustration. "That's right. She's told me all about you. You may have been important to her at one time, but not anymore."

A creak from the steps draws our attention. Tillie is standing halfway down the staircase with her brow furrowed. She looks exhausted but there's also no mistaking her anger.

"You both need to stop," she says, almost too quietly to be heard. "Isaiah, I appreciate you sticking around to make sure I'm okay, but maybe you should go."

Shocked at her words, I look from her to the cocky expression of Henry and back again. When Tillie says nothing more, offers no explanation for her sudden change of heart, I stride toward the steps and make my way to her.

"If that's what you want," I say just before leaning in and kissing her on the cheek. "I'm just a phone call or text message away," I whisper in her ear.

Tillie gives a tight nod and I retrace my steps and go to the front door. As the door shuts behind me, I hear Henry question Tillie about my presence and my lips tip up into a satisfied grin when she cops an attitude with him.

I shove my hands in my pockets and take my time walking to my parent's house. It's a long walk as Tillie lives on the west side of the property and they live on the east side. I use the time to think about the last forty-eight hours.

During the flight home, I prepared myself for as many scenarios as I could regarding Tillie's reaction to me. I had a plan for every single one. If she refused to talk to me, I'd make a pest of myself until she caved. If she was happy to see me, I'd be grateful and not bring up the past unless she did. If she wanted to beat the hell out of me, I'd let her. On and on and on, I planned.

What I didn't plan on was Tillie being attacked and her needing me. Sure, she asked me to leave this morning, but she'd wanted me there when it mattered. Images of Tillie's bruised face surface and I clench my fists in my pockets. I know the basics of what happened to her, but I don't know *why* it happened.

Is the Uber driver someone she knows? Was it a random attack? Related to her work? There are so many possibilities and I vow to look into every single one until I find the guy and make him pay for hurting her.

My thoughts shift to the reason I'm home. When I woke up in the hospital in Italy, where the military had transported me, I couldn't remember why I was there. My brain was so foggy, that details were impossible to recall. When I asked a nurse about it, she filled in some of the gaps. Words like 'bombing' and 'casualties' penetrated the ringing in my ears as she talked, and I remember pain like I've never experienced. Not physical. No, the pain that day was all emotional. It was an agony that the IV pain meds couldn't relieve.

"Isaiah!"

I whirl around, my fists raised and ready to strike. My dad stands there with his hands up to block his face from my reaction. There is no fear on his face, only sad recognition.

"It's just me, son," he says as he lowers his hands. "It's just me."

"Jesus," I mumble and drop my own arms as if they're heavy lead weights. "Sorry, Pops."

"No need to apologize." His eyes search mine. "Have you talked to anyone about that?"

"About what?" There's a defensive quality to my tone. One that I can't help.

"The PTSD you're sporting."

My body stiffens at the mention of my weakness, my cross to bear for what I failed to do.

"Did you, when you got out?" I counter.

"Not as much as I should have," he replies.

My PTSD is the last thing I want to talk about, especially with my father. He may understand exactly what I'm going through, but if he sees any sort of weakness in me, he may second guess the decision to make me president. Besides, he doesn't need the stress.

"Did you need something?" I ask in an effort to change the subject.

"Yeah." His eyes search mine. "First, how's Tillie doing this morning?"

"She's got Henry, so she's good." I can taste the jealousy, the bitterness. It's like acid on my tongue and I swallow past it. "Next question."

"No more questions. But you're needed at the main house."

"For?" I want to go home, or at least to my temporary home at my parent's house, and shower. I want to wash away the unwanted emotions coursing through me. I want to be alone.

"You're the goddamn president now. You need to start thinking like it," he snaps. "After what happened to Tillie, the club needs to know what you plan to do. They need to know that you're taking this seriously. You need to discuss, with the club, what to do about Tillie's attack, run down the facts, the ones we know, and come up with a plan."

"Without Tillie there?"

Discussing her ordeal without her being present feels wrong, out of line with everything I remember about how the Brotherhood handles its business. We've never shied away from the hard stuff, the stuff that the law couldn't handle. And we've never kept a member out of the loop, especially when it involves them.

"For now." He glances over my shoulder in the direction of Tillie's house. "Besides, you said Henry's at her place. Give her a bit of time before we call her in."

My dad gives me one last long look before he turns away and strides in the direction of the main house. I stare after him for a moment and then force my feet to come unglued from their spot and follow.

"Hey, son." I turn toward the voice and smile when I see

Griffin, my dad's best friend and the former Vice President of the club. "How is she?"

"Don't ask," my father says from behind him. "Touchy subject."

"Ah, okay." Griffin grins but his lips flatten out when he sees the look on my face. "Right. Well…"

"Leave the poor kid alone." Brie, Griffin's wife and a founding member of the club lays a hand on my bicep. "How are *you* doing, Isaiah? I know this isn't the homecoming you wanted."

"I'm fine," I snap, uncomfortable with the attention being on me. "Is this a gossip session or business? Because I've got things to do."

"Isaiah," Isabelle barks from the table behind me. "Quit being a dick."

I roll my eyes and make my way to the seat next to my sister. I realize what I'm doing and switch directions to take my new place at the head of the table. My dad sits at the other end, with my mom just to his left. Liam sits to my right and the rest of the voting members making up the long sides of the worn wood.

A hushed silence settles over the room and my skin crawls. I don't like the quiet. Not like I used to. It doesn't calm me as it once did, doesn't envelop me in security. All the quiet does now is give me the opportunity to think about shit that I'd rather not think about.

"Let's get this meeting rolling." Liam's voice booms through the room and eases the tension in my shoulders.

"As you all know, one of our own was attacked last night," I start. All eyes shift to Aiden, no doubt trying to gauge his reaction to the attack on his daughter. "The only information we have is what Tillie could provide. That it was her Uber driver and a name, which law enforcement has learned was fake. Does anyone know if she has any enemies?" My gaze cuts to Isabelle because I figure if anyone would know, it'd be her.

Everyone looks at me as if I'm an idiot, but Isabelle is the one to respond. "Of course, she's got enemies. She's an attorney for victims of domestic violence. Not only does her own career put her in harm's way, but being a part of this club does, as well."

"Do any of her clients stand out? Have there been any threats? Has anyone considered—"

"Slow down, Isaiah," Aiden admonishes. "One thing at a time."

I take a deep breath to try to do as advised. It's harder than I thought being the president and keeping my personal shit in check.

"There haven't been any threats that we're aware of," my dad says and looks to Isabelle for confirmation.

"She hasn't told me about any. I'm pretty sure if she was scared of someone or if something were going on, I'd know."

"What about any of the club's clients? Anyone have someone that stands out as a possibility?" I look around the room and everyone shakes their heads. "Okay."

My dad speaks up from his seat as he leans his elbows on the table. "I think we need to consider that this could have been totally random."

"It's never random!" I lunge to my feet and my chair crashes to the ground behind me. "You can't—"

"Sit down." My father's tone is laced with steel. I stare him down, both of us glaring. "Isaiah, sit the fuck down."

I glare for another moment before turning around and righting my chair so I can sit. Rage boils my blood. Once again, I'm being called out in front of everyone. Add that to the fact that it appears that we've got nothing on what happened to Tillie, or who attacked her, and I'm teetering on the ragged edge of sanity.

"I met with the Sheriff this morning," Liam says. "He released the photo they had of the driver and Griffin's running it through his facial recognition software."

"Why aren't they running it themselves?" I ask, frustrated.

"They are. But you know as well as I do that our small-town department doesn't have a ton of resources." Griffin shrugs. "My software is better."

"Keep us posted on that." I look to Aiden, the only other person in the room that appears as tightly wound as I feel. "Aiden, I'm gonna need you to talk to Tillie, get her to see reason and accept protection."

"Have you met my daughter?" Aiden says with a touch of humor. "We tried at the hospital and she wasn't having any of it. Says she can handle herself."

"She's always been stubborn. I say we don't give her a choice in the matter."

"You know that's not how this works. We don't force our protection on anyone. We help them when they want it."

"This is such bullshit."

All heads whip in the direction of the door. Tillie is standing there with her arms crossed over her chest and her battered face blazing with barely concealed fury. Most would look at her, this woman who is no bigger than a minute with curly blonde hair and bright blue eyes, and not be afraid. We aren't most people. We know better.

"I can't believe I don't get a say in this," Tillie says as she strides to her seat and yanks it out from the table. "What the hell? Despite evidence to the contrary, I can take care of myself."

"Peanut, we—"

"Don't call me Peanut," Tillie snaps at her dad. "Not here."

"Fine. *Tillie,*" Aiden starts over. "No one is saying you can't take care of yourself. But you were attacked. And we can't just sit back and ignore that. Dammit, *I* won't sit back and ignore it."

Tillie's face softens as Aiden speaks. She's always been a daddy's girl and the fact that she's twenty-six hasn't changed that. It just means she's a daddy's girl with an attitude.

As if willing away the rest of the conversation, Tillie takes a deep breath and blows it out. She turns her head to take in everyone at the table. When her gaze lands on me, her face becomes expressionless.

"Don't do this, Isaiah," Tillie pleads. "Don't take away my choices."

Without taking my eyes off of her, I quickly rethink my strategy and say, "I'd like to put Tillie's protection to a vote." She opens her mouth to protest and I raise a hand to stop her. "Now that she's present, I think it's only fair that she gets a say in this."

Tillie's mouth slams shut and her eyes widen, almost comically. She clearly wasn't expecting me to include her in this decision. This decision that affects her so profoundly.

"All those in favor of Tillie being under around the clock protection, let your vote be heard."

Tillie is the only 'no' as votes are cast. She's going to be protected, whether she wants it or not. I just need her to see things my way.

"Tillie, what do you suggest then? I want you safe and I'm not willing," I pause and rethink my approach. "*We* aren't willing to gamble with your life. So, what would make you feel better about having around the clock protection?"

She looks at me and the look on her face says it all. It's a look I know very well, one she's clearly perfected even more since I left eight years ago. It's the look she gets when she's about to screw you as completely as she thinks you're screwing her.

"I'll take the protection, *Prez,* but I want it to be you." Her smile widens and if it was possible, I'd say it looks even more evil genius. "I have a spare bedroom as you're aware. You don't have your own place." She folds her arms over her chest, pushing her tits up even higher. "Stay at my house and I'll take the protection. It's a win-win situation."

Well, fuck.

12

TILLIE

"You can't be serious?"

I continue to stare out the passenger window of Henry's Mercedes, catching sight of Isaiah riding Nyx in the side mirror. The rumble of the Harley is a comforting sound. Much more enjoyable than Henry's obvious distaste for my protection detail.

"Henry, it's not like I have a choice. Isaiah is the president now and what he says goes."

I don't like the way the partial truth rolls off my tongue. If Henry knew that I set the rules for my protection, he'd be furious. Although, his fury is not nearly as scary as Isaiah's.

"Honey, I know you have a long history with Isaiah, but are you sure there's not still some unresolved feelings there?"

Of course, he'd ask that question. I wish I could put Henry's mind at ease. I wish I could tell him what he wants to hear without the guilt and soul-crushing pain that the answer causes me. But the truth of the matter is, there are feelings there. All kinds of feelings, not all good.

"I guess that's my answer."

Finally, I look away from the window and toward the

man who has been my rock for the last year. The man who somehow worked his way past all of my defenses and made me see that Isaiah Mallory may not be the only man I can love.

"Henry, I don't—"

"Please don't spout some bullshit lie, Tillie."

My eyebrows shoot up at his use of a swear word. Henry doesn't cuss. Not ever. He tolerates it from me, but to him, cussing is 'trashy', so hearing him say bullshit is surprising. And probably a pretty good indication of how frazzled Isaiah has him.

"I wasn't going to lie to you." I reach out and rest my hand on his arm, disappointed when my touch isn't met with corded muscle. Frustration courses through me, because until a few days ago, that wouldn't have even fazed me. "I was going to say that you're right. There are definitely some unresolved issues between Isaiah and me. But that has nothing to do with the protection."

Henry glances in the rearview mirror and groans. "Whatever you say."

Anger hits me fast and hard. I don't like being accused of lying, especially by someone who is supposed to love me, trust me. Besides, doesn't he get that I've been through hell and the last thing I need is his shit?

"Just drive."

The last ten minutes to my house are quiet, except for the rumble of Isaiah's Harley behind us. I can't stop myself from looking in the side mirror, despite my best efforts. What the fuck was I thinking when I told him to stay at my house? Obviously, I wasn't.

"What the hell?"

When Henry pulls into my driveway, I'm lost in thought, so it takes a minute for his words to register. A Ford F-250 is parked in front of the porch steps and Liam, along with Jace and Noah, appear to be unloading furniture and carrying it inside. There's also a moving pod sitting in the yard and if I have to guess, I'd say it's the stuff that Isaiah had shipped home.

I recognize the dresser that's still sitting in the bed of the truck, as the one from Isaiah's bedroom at his parent's house. I swallow back a groan at the conflict I know is about to start. I flinch when my door is flung open.

Isaiah leans his head inside the car. "Gonna sit here all day or are you coming in?"

"Jesus, you scared me," I snap.

"Sorry."

Isaiah steps back and allows me room to get out. I look over my shoulder to see Henry getting out on the driver's side, a scowl on his face.

"Is this really necessary? I can see to Tillie's safety." Henry yanks his sunglasses off of his face and tosses them on his seat before closing the door.

"Look, I don't know how things have worked for the last eight years, but I'm in charge now and I'll handle club business the way I see fit." Isaiah steps around the hood of the Mercedes to stand toe to toe with Henry. "You got a problem with that pretty boy, you can leave."

"Isaiah!" I shout, anger bubbling over. "Back the fuck off."

"It's okay, Tillie," Henry says with his hand out to stop my advance. "I can handle this. I'm sure his bark is worse than his bite."

Isaiah barks out a laugh. "I wouldn't be so sure about that."

"Quit comparing dick sizes and help unload the rest of *your* shit," Liam calls from the porch.

"Guess you'll have to hear all about my bite from Tillie." Isaiah turns away from Henry, winks at me, and then makes his way to the truck to help.

"Tillie, I've tried to be civil, I really have, but I don't think that man has a single civilized bone in his body."

"I'm sorry my attack is causing you so much grief," I snap, unable to control my temper any longer. I rub my temples, trying to get rid of the growing migraine. "Look, do we have to do this right now? I don't want to fight with you."

"I don't want to fight either." Henry steps up to me and grabs my hands, not showing any thought for the still-healing wounds. "But Tillie, you're gonna have to make a choice here."

I search his eyes, wondering if he's serious. Apparently, he is. "I love you, but I can't compete with a history as long as the one you have with him." Henry drops my hands and shoves his in his pockets. "You've got some decisions to make. I'll wait, but not long."

He places a light kiss on my cheek and turns to get back in his Mercedes. As I watch him drive away, two things happen. One, tears well in my eyes, and two, a crushing weight lifts from my shoulders.

I swipe at the wetness on my cheeks, wincing when I rub the bruises and abrasions. I haven't taken the pain medication like I'm supposed to because I hate how they make me feel, so everything I do hurts. If Isaiah knew that, he'd hover even more, so I try to pull myself together and do my best to ignore the pain.

When I turn around to head into the house, Isaiah is standing on the porch, staring. *Fuck. How much did he see... or hear?* I cautiously make my way to the steps. His mouth opens as if he's going to say something, but I don't give him a chance and instead, shove past him and go inside and directly upstairs to my bedroom.

I know Isaiah will follow me, but I still don't lock the door. I tell myself it's because he knows how to pick a lock and if he didn't, he'd just bust the door down and that's not something I want to deal with at the moment. Even I recognize the lie in that thought. If I'm honest with myself, there's a part of me—a teeny-tiny part, way deep down—that wants him to follow me, wants him to come in and make everything better.

I startle at the soft tap of knuckles on the door. "Tillie, is everything okay?"

A small smile plays on my lips at Isaiah's voice. Isaiah is nothing, if not predictable.

He wasn't so predictable when he chose to go to BUD/S training. You'd do well to remember that.

"Tillie?" His voice is a little more insistent. "I know you're in there."

I sit on the bed and fold my legs under me as my smile grows.

"Dammit, Tillie."

He's getting angry now. My grin slips a bit but judging by the scowl on his face when he pushes the door open, not enough.

"Sure, come on in," I say sarcastically.

Isaiah tilts his head at my attitude and takes a few steps toward the bed. "Where'd Henry go?" His eyes narrow. "And why were you crying? What did he do?"

I sigh at the way his tone changes from annoyance to concern. "He left."

"No shit, Til," Isaiah says, stepping closer. "But why? One minute I was flipping him shit and he was flipping it right back and the next he's leaving and you're crying."

"It's nothing."

I stand and try to walk past him, not wanting to have this conversation. Isaiah reaches out and grabs my arm, careful not to hurt me. He shifts to stand in front of me and pins me with his gaze.

"What. Happened?" he demands.

I glare back at him. "He had some work to do."

"Bullshit." Isaiah counters. "You've never lied to me before. Why are you starting now?"

He really has no fucking clue. I *have* lied to him… when it mattered most. I breathe in deeply through my nose, let the air out past my lips.

"Henry thinks there's something here." I swing my hand back and forth between us and Isaiah's eyebrows rise. "He said he'd give me time to figure it out, but that he won't wait long."

Several minutes pass as we stare at each other. It's impossible to miss the way his pupils dilate or the way my breathing changes with each passing second. The effect he has on me is unmistakable and I realize I've made a grave error in judgment thinking I'd be okay with him under the same roof.

I break eye contact and look toward the door. "I'm gonna go see if Liam or the guys want anything to drink."

I get as far as the top of the staircase before Isaiah is on my heels.

"Why does he think there's something between us?"

I stop in my tracks and whirl on him, fury slamming into me like a lead weight.

"Are you fucking kidding me?" I shout, not giving a damn who hears me. "You've spent every second since you've been home doing your best to make him feel like you're staking your claim. He knows about our history. He knows *me*. He's not a stupid man, Isaiah."

"Is he right?"

"What?"

"You heard me, Til." Isaiah rubs the back of his neck. "Is he right about us? About there being something between us?"

All of my anger leaves as quickly as it arrived, and my

body seems to deflate. "That's the million-dollar question, isn't it?"

"It's a pretty simple question."

"No, Isaiah, it's not a simple question." I search his eyes and realize he really believes it's simple. I shake my head. "It's as complicated a question as it can get."

"Do you wanna know what I think?"

Wrinkles crease my forehead as I think about that. Do I? Do I really want to know? Yeah, I do. I give a tight nod.

"I think it's been a long eight years. I think there are feelings involved for both of us." He pauses and cups my cheek. "And I think you're scared shitless to make yourself vulnerable again because you're afraid I'm not gonna stick around." I involuntarily lean into his touch. "I hate to break it to you, Til, but I'm not going anywhere. And I'm going to prove to you that we belong together. We always have."

13

ISAIAH

"Prez, are you even listening?"

I whip my head to the right and fight a groan at the annoyed look on Liam's face. We're sitting in the library at the main house, discussing cases that were being worked when I was transitioned in as president. There's so much information to catch up on from the last eight years. I've been at Tillie's house for a week and rarely am I without a file in my hand or my laptop open in front of me. Granted, I've needed the distraction. Being in such close proximity to the one woman who revs me up every second she's breathing has tried my resolve in ways I never thought I'd be tested.

"I'm listening," I finally reply.

"And…" Liam stares at me waiting for a response. "Jesus, you weren't listening. Where the hell are you today?"

"I'm right here."

I turn away from his glare and snag two beers from the mini fridge. He's not wrong about my mind being elsewhere but I do know what he was talking about. I should be with Tillie, making sure she is okay, but Adam is keeping tabs on her today so I can focus on club business.

"Here." I thrust a beer at Liam and he quickly twists the cap off and takes a few swallows. "What's the plan for Daryl Sloops? It seems like the first visit scared him a bit, but I don't like the anonymous letters that Rachel keeps getting."

The look of surprise on Liam's face that I was following what he was saying is as comical as it is annoying.

"Jace and I are keeping a close eye on that. Rachel seems to be more comfortable with him than me, so he's sticking close."

"Have we made any headway on who's sending the letters?"

"Jace is pretty sure he's tracked them back to the ex but until we can confirm it, we're holding off on a second visit to Daryl."

"Keep me posted," I remind him. "And if you need anything from me, let me know."

"You know I will."

I give a tight nod. "Jace seems like he's got his shit together. So do the other new members. At least, from what I've seen."

"They're all great and have their own specialties that they bring to the table. As for Jace… he's quiet. I don't know much about his backstory. He pretty much keeps to himself." Liam leans back in his chair. "I will say, other than you, there's no one else I'd rather have fighting next to me."

"Good to know." I finish off my beer and toss the empty bottle in the trash. After a glance at the clock, I realize that Tillie should be getting home soon. "Anything else we need to discuss?"

"Yeah. How are things going with Tillie?"

I swallow back the groan that threatens to roll up my throat and try to make things sound like they aren't a giant shit show. "Good. You know how she is. A pain in the ass and too damn stubborn for her own good."

"Right." Liam chuckles. "How's she feeling though? Is she healing up okay?"

"Yeah, things in that department are all good. Bruises are slowly fading. Abrasions are healing." I run my hand over the beard I'm allowing to grow now that I'm out of the military. "She has nightmares though and refuses to talk to anyone about it."

"I'm sure you can relate." Liam's expression turns serious.

"What's that supposed to mean?"

"Nothing, man." Liam raises his hands in a gesture of surrender. "It's just, I know what our parents went through after the military. Shit, it's why we're all here, why the BRB exists. Just figured it's probably pretty similar for you."

Liam turns away from me and heads toward the door. Just before he steps across the threshold, I call out to him.

"Thanks, Liam."

He looks over his shoulder and nods once. "Any time." He stares at me a moment before continuing. "I know you're not a talker, but I'm here if you decide you want to. Better yet, talk to Tillie about it. She's always been who you relied on when shit hit the fan. You might be surprised that she can still be that person."

Liam walks out of the room and I'm left with my own swirling thoughts. Can I talk to Tillie? *Should* I talk to her, tell her everything that happened?

No, not yet.

Comfortable with my decision to keep my own crap buried and focus on Tillie, I shut down my laptop and pack everything up to head back to Tillie's place. When I exit the main house, I see Tillie's BMW heading toward her house, followed by Adam on his Harley. Adam waves when he sees me on the porch, and I wave back.

While I want to get to Tillie as quickly as possible, I know that Adam is with her, so I take a slight detour and go to a spot that I've always gone to clear my head. Elephant Hill is a peaceful place with tragic beginnings and it's exactly what I need right now.

I park Nyx at the bottom of the hill and climb to the top and sit to look out over the expanse of land below. Growing up, I was always told that this was where my parents had a huge turning point in their relationship. They never went into specifics but every time I come here, I feel a sense of peace, a sense of being right where I belong.

I lean back in the grass and use my arms as a resting place for my head. I stare at the sky and remember the last time I was here. It was with Tillie, a week before I left for basic training. She'd made me promise that day that we'd always be together. I knew when I made that promise that I was leaving. Hell, so did she. But I didn't know that there'd be an eight-year gap from when I left to when I saw her again.

My thoughts shift to graduation day and the look on Tillie's face when she opened that hotel room door. The second I'd laid eyes on her I'd wanted to change my mind, do what I promised her I'd do, and pray that I'd be stationed somewhere she'd like to move to. Instead, I stood there like the stupid fool I was and let her support my decision. And then I fucking thanked her.

Clouds roll by and I track their movement across the blue expanse above me. My phone vibrates in my pocket and I pull it out to look at the text.

Tillie: Where r u?

I type out a quick text to tell her I'd be home soon. Just as I'm about to shove my phone back into my jeans, it vibrates again.

Tillie: Sent Adam home. Henry is here.

I scramble to my feet and jog to my bike. I may not know what the hell I'm doing when it comes to Tillie and whatever may or may not be between us, but I sure as shit know I don't want her alone with Henry. And what the hell is Adam doing leaving before I get there? I make a mental note to talk to him about that next time I see him.

I break every speed limit to get to Tillie's house. On winding country roads, it's probably not the smartest thing but I don't care. I don't want Henry to have a chance to sweet talk Tillie into staying in the relationship.

When I pull into the driveway, I heave a sigh that's a mixture of relief and frustration when I see the Mercedes parked by the garage. I head inside and see both of them sitting on the couch, deep in conversation.

"Hey," I say, reveling in satisfaction when Henry jumps.

Tillie rolls her eyes. "You didn't have to rush home."

"Of course, he did," Henry huffs. "He doesn't trust me. Although I don't know why. I am your boyfriend."

"Are you?" I grate out. "Because a boyfriend wouldn't leave her unprotected."

"She wasn't unprotected," Henry shouts. "She's had you and the club."

"Shouldn't matter who else she's had," I counter. I step up to the back of the couch, just behind Tillie. "If you loved her, you'd have been here, no matter what. If you gave a shit about her, you'd fight for her. Not run off like a little bitch because you're afraid of a little competition."

"Dammit, stop!" Tillie yells, jumping up from the couch and whirling around to face me. "I'm right fucking here. Quit talking about me like I'm not."

"I know exactly where you are," I growl, pinning her with my stare. "At all times, I know where the fuck you are." Anger battles common sense as I seethe. "It's my job to know."

"Yes, it's your job." Henry stands and puts an arm around

Tillie's waist. I don't miss the way she flinches at his touch. "And I have an important job, as a prosecutor. I don't have time to ride around on a hunk of metal and pretend that I'm working."

The sound of flesh on flesh echoes in the air when Tillie's hand connects with Henry's cheek. Shock settles into Henry's expression and he takes a step away from her. Tillie shakes her hand out as if in pain and I rush around to make sure she's okay.

She doesn't resist when I pick her hand up to inspect it. "You okay?"

"I'm fine." She yanks her hand out of my hold and glares at me. "Is that all I am to you? A job?"

I glance beyond her at Henry and see the hurt that flashes in his eyes. As much as I dislike the guy, I've caused enough damage and if Tillie cares about him then I want her decision to be made for the right reasons and not because she's pissed off. "Why don't you handle things with your boyfriend? We can talk later."

She twists her head to take in the man she's called boyfriend for the last year. "You need to leave," she informs him, no apology in her tone.

"Tillie, honey, I'm sorry," Henry pleads. "You know I love everything about you and your family. I didn't mean what I said."

"Yeah, you did." She sighs and drops to sit on the couch. "Clearly, you have no idea what is important to me. You certainly have no idea what I'm all about if you could say something like that."

"But—"

"We're done, Henry." She drops her chin into the palms of her hands as her elbows rest on her knees. "I'll have one of the guys bring you any of your stuff I come across but right now, I need you to leave. And don't come back. Please."

My heart cracks at the tremble in Tillie's voice. I've caused this woman so much pain, so much misery, and here we are again, my lack of thought smack dab in the middle of her suffering. Ignoring the way her pain radiates off of her in waves, I walk toward the door and tug it open.

"You heard her." I direct my statement at Henry. When he's right in front of me, I say, "For what it's worth, I am sorry. I don't give a shit about you, but I love her and I'm sorry that causes her any amount of heartache."

Henry shakes his head and when he turns back around toward Tillie, I grab his arm to stop him. "Just go."

He rushes through the doorway and all is silent until he peels out of the driveway, spraying up gravel and dust. The sound of Tillie's crying reaches me and I go to her, unsure of how to make it better.

Tillie looks up at me with luminous eyes, mascara streaking her cheeks, and her bottom lip quivering. Unable to stay away, I sit next to her and pull her onto my lap. I expect her to resist, to get angry so when she settles into my body, I'm shocked.

"I'm sorry, Til," I whisper against her hair. I hold her, rock her, soothe her, and will do it for however long it takes. And I apologize again. For her break-up, for her attack, for every ounce of pain, I've ever caused her. I apologize for it all, over and over again.

"I'm so damn sorry."

14

TILLIE

I let out a groan as I roll over in bed and slap a hand over my alarm clock to stop the incessant beeping that pulled me from sleep. I blink a few times to allow my vision to adjust to the morning sun streaming through my windows and stifle a yawn. My body still aches from the attack and my broken ribs need more time to heal but I'm slowly starting to feel normal again.

I toss the covers off of me and sit up to stretch. The strong smell of coffee permeates the air and I make quick work of throwing on my robe over the boxers and tank I slept in. When I open my bedroom door, I hear a deep voice and it takes a moment for it to register that it's Isaiah talking on the phone.

"Thanks for letting me know," he says to whoever is on the other end of the line. "Gotta go."

Isaiah makes no move to turn around and face me. He shoves his cell into his back pocket, drawing my attention to the way his ass looks in his jeans. He's not wearing a shirt or socks and shoes, and my mouth goes dry at the tattoos that cover his back in a beautiful swirl of ink and intricate designs.

"Coffee's ready."

"Huh?" I try to swallow but fail miserably.

"The coffee," he says as he finally turns around. The front view is equally impressive. "It's ready."

"Um…" I lick my lips. "Okay."

"Til?"

I raise my head and take in the grin on his face. "What?" My tone is harsher than I intend but he's such a distraction and I'm angry with myself for being caught eye-fucking him.

"Do you want some coffee?"

"Yes." I take the mug he offers me and step up to the fridge.

"Already added your creamer," Isaiah says. "And your sugar."

"Oh." I slink back to the table and drop down into a chair. "Thanks."

"No problem." He crosses his arms over his chest and the tattoo of the American flag on his right pec seems to ripple with the movement. "How'd you sleep?"

I shrug. "Okay, I guess." I don't want to admit that, after he held me and tucked me into bed, I slept like the dead. At least, until I heard him yelling. I'd gotten up to see what was going on and realized that he was having a nightmare. Part of me wanted to wake him, reassure him and remind him of where he was, but the chicken shit part of me won out and I returned to my own bed. "You?" I ask, even though I know the answer.

"Slept great." I don't have a chance to confront the lie because he changes the subject quickly. "What's on the agenda today?" he asks, turning away and putting some bread into the toaster.

"I've got a few things to do around the house but then I plan on spending the day at the shelter." I take a sip of my coffee, savoring the sugary sweet caffeine. "You?"

"I'll be with you." His tone is laced with sarcasm. "Obviously."

"No presidential duties to take care of today?" I mock.

"Already took care of them. Jace is still working with Ms. Sloops. Noah and Adam are meeting with a potential client and Liam is meeting with the sheriff to see if they've got any news on your case."

At the mention of my attack, my stomach churns and my muscles clench. Isaiah either has a much better understanding of me than I think or he's extremely observant because he immediately rushes to my side and grazes my cheek with his fingertips.

"Nobody is gonna hurt you, Til." His voice is husky and wraps around me like crushed velvet. "Not on my watch."

"You don't know that." I lock eyes with him and start to get lost in the blue-gray depths. In an effort to put some distance between us, I stand up and force my gaze to the window over the kitchen sink. "I know I agreed to protection, but it can't go on forever, Isaiah."

"It can go on as long as it has to."

"That's what I'm afraid of," I mumble under my breath.

"What?"

"Nothing." I make my way out of the kitchen and call over my shoulder, "I'm gonna go grab a shower."

Isaiah doesn't respond but I didn't really expect him to. I'm just grateful he isn't following me to sit on the bathroom floor to protect me from some invisible threat.

I adjust the water temperature and when it's as hot as I can stand it, I step under the spray and slick my hair back to wet it. As I wash my body, my fingers run over the scars on my thighs and my mind drifts back in time to the moment the first one appeared.

It had been the one-year anniversary of when Isaiah left. Against my better judgment, I'd written him a letter and begged him to meet me at the same hotel that we'd stayed at for his graduation. Like a stupid girl, I thought he'd miss me enough to do whatever it took to get there. So, I packed a bag and took off, not telling anyone where I went.

When I arrived at the hotel, Isaiah wasn't there, and again, I used my powers of persuasion on myself and believed that he would show up. I put on the jeans he bought me because he said they made my ass look great and a revealing leather halter top. I primped and preened until I looked like every man's wet dream.

Four hours passed before I even started to doubt my plan. Another two went by before the tears started. I let one more hour tick along and then it set in. Isaiah wasn't coming. I raided the mini-bar and locked myself in the bathroom for the remaining hours that I had the room.

A loud thump against the door jolts me from my melancholy memories and I almost slip on the sudsy shower floor.

"Tillie!" Isaiah's tone sounds urgent and his pounding on the door is so hard I'm worried he's going to break the damn thing. "Tillie, are you okay?"

"Stop pounding!" I yell at him. When he stops, I breathe a sigh of relief. "What the hell do you want?"

"Are you okay? I've been knocking for five minutes."

Shocked by that information, I realize I must have been more lost in my head than I thought. "I'm fine. Did you need something?"

"You've got visitors."

Who the hell is visiting? I kicked Henry out last night so I doubt it's him and the only other people who stop by are club members, all of whom Isaiah could just entertain while I finish up.

"I'll be down in a few minutes."

I quickly rinse off and make quick work of drying off. I race to my bedroom to throw some clothes on. I don't bother to put on makeup or do my hair. I can do that after the 'visitor' leaves.

When I descend the steps, I halt halfway down. Isaiah is pacing and he doesn't appear happy. The sheriff is standing behind the couch and Henry is next to him. Red hot rage simmers just beneath the surface and I take the remaining steps two at a time, only stopping when I'm directly next to Henry.

All common sense flees as I grab his arm and whirl him around to face me. His eyes are wide with surprise. "What the fuck are you doing here?"

The sheriff turns around, clearly having not heard me approach. "Miss Winters, I asked him to come."

"I'm sorry Sheriff, but I don't give a damn. He's not welcome in my home."

"I'm not welcome but he is?" Henry sounds offended and nods his head to indicate Isaiah.

"This isn't the time or place for personal crap," the Sheriff interjects before I can respond. He refocuses his attention on me. "Miss Winters, I tried to call you, but your phone went straight to voicemail, so I decided to stop by instead. Mr. Stringer is with me because of official business. I'm sorry if his presence upsets you but it couldn't be avoided."

"What official business, Sheriff?" Isaiah asks from across the room. "It must be something big if you couldn't wait until your appointment with Liam."

"The Uber driver was caught," Henry blurts out.

My knees threaten to buckle and my head spins. I never

dreamed he'd be caught so quickly, especially since Griffin hadn't found anything. He's the best hacker and computer wizard I know and can find just about anyone.

"Miss Winters, why don't we sit down so we can discuss a few things?"

The Sheriff grips my elbow and guides me around the couch to sit down. Henry tries to sit next to me but when I glare at him, he remains standing. Isaiah, however, has no such issue. The cushion dips under his weight and he puts an arm around my shoulders.

"How? When? Where?" So many questions bombard me, and I spit them out as quickly as I can.

"He tried to attack another woman in the early morning hours. Unfortunately for him, that woman is an undercover FBI agent that was sent to assist in the investigation."

"Wait…" I try to process the information. "Why was the FBI assisting?"

"When you were attacked, the MO and suspect description were entered into a national database. It matched a serial rapist case that the FBI was working on because the suspect has crossed numerous state lines."

"Jesus," Isaiah groans. "How many women has he attacked?"

"Thirteen that the FBI is aware of. He always kills his victims following the rape." The Sheriff's face softens. "At least, until you. For whatever reason, he left you alive. The FBI was fairly certain that he'd stick around to finish the job and put an undercover agent in place in case he decided to find another target in the meantime."

"Holy shit." My heart is pounding so hard I fear that they'll be able to see the beat through my shirt. As the reality of what could have happened settles in, I lean into Isaiah and his arm tightens around me. "I'm glad you caught him but

I'm still not real clear on why he's here." I nod at Henry but don't look at him.

"As an attorney, you know that it's critical to get the victim's statement and to review all the facts as quickly as possible. Mr. Stringer is going to be prosecuting the case and I wanted him to talk with you now, rather than wait until the details begin to fade over time."

"Tillie," Henry starts. "I asked for this case. I know you think I don't care about you, but I do. I want to do my part to put this bastard behind bars."

I look at Isaiah and take in his clenched jaw, the way his pulse jumps at his neck. He doesn't like the idea any more than I do. But I'm afraid I don't have a choice. I know how busy the prosecutor's office is and once a case is claimed by one of the attorneys, they're not likely to be able to pass it off to anyone else. Henry knew that and made sure that I wouldn't have an excuse to not see him again. *Asshole.*

"Fine. But I'll come into the office for anything relating to the case. And Isaiah will be with me." I practically dare Henry with my glare to argue. He wisely chooses to keep his mouth shut.

"We'll look at our schedules and call your office to set up an appointment." Isaiah twists that knife just a bit further then he looks at the sheriff. "Do you need anything else today?"

"No, no. That'll be all." The sheriff seems flustered by the tension in the room, but I don't care. After Henry's comment yesterday, he made the decision to call it quits easy and I don't want him in my house. "Here's my card. Call if you need anything." He holds out his business card to Isaiah and I snatch it, more anger rising at having been overlooked.

Isaiah stands and shows both of them to the door, flipping the lock when they leave. I hear a thump and turn in time to see him lean his head back against the wall. I take a minute to enjoy the view when he can't see me.

"Does this mean what I think it means?"

"Does what mean what—"

"You not wanting douchebag in your house," Isaiah interrupts and stands up straight to pin me with his stare. "Does that mean I have a shot?"

"Why would you think that?" I cock my head to the side, genuinely curious where he came up with that logic.

"Because he gave you an ultimatum. Obviously, there's something between us and with him out of the way I need to know if I actually have a chance at a relationship with you or if I'm wasting my time." He breaks eye contact and drops his chin. "I don't think I can take another hit right now, Til."

How is it possible for a man to go from controlled rage to cocky confidence to pitiful insecurity in the span of twenty minutes? And why is it that the pitiful insecurity is what I'm drawn to the most?

Because you want to know what caused it. You want him to trust you enough with his story. And you want to trust him enough to share all of yours with him.

"Isaiah, I…"

"What?"

"I don't know." I climb over the back of the couch and close the distance between us to rest my hands on his chest. "I need time. Fuck, *we* need time. You just got back and we both have a lot of shit to deal with. I just… I need time."

Isaiah wraps his arms around me and pulls me into him. Our bodies fit as perfectly as I remember, better even. I breathe in his scent, the same scent that I used to sniff like I was huffing nail polish because it's so intoxicating.

"I'll give you time, Til. I'll give you all the time you need. But I have one condition."

I tip my head back to look at him and narrow my eyes. "What's that," I ask with suspicion.

"I'm staying here while you take that time."

The stubborn part of me wants to argue, wants to shout at him that he can't just take over my life, but my heart, the same heart that beats for him, shuts that thought down.

"Okay."

15

ISAIAH

"I forgot what that felt like."

Tillie isn't the only one. I haven't had a woman's arms wrapped around me on Nyx in eight years. No one other than Isabelle and she doesn't count. Now that I think about it, Tillie is the only female I've ever had on the back of Nyx.

I'm transfixed by the grin on Tillie's face and the way she finger combs her windblown blonde curls. My cock twitches when her shirt rides up and a sliver of her stomach is revealed. Her jeans sit low on her hips and hug her thighs in such a way that would make any man envious of the worn denim.

"Me too." Somehow, I manage to push the words past my lips.

"C'mon."

Tillie turns and starts to walk toward the employee entrance of the shelter where we picked up Carla. It takes me a few seconds to force my feet to move because as tantalizing as the front of Tillie is, the view as she walks away is even more hypnotizing.

When I finally step through the door, Tillie is already talking to a woman that I don't recognize. Based on the expression on the woman's face and Tillie's body language, the conversation is not about rainbows and puppies.

"I just don't know what to do," the woman says in a worried whisper. "She refuses to stay here because of the kids but I'm worried that the next time he shows up at the house, he'll kill her."

"Who's gonna kill who?" I ask, inserting myself into the conversation.

Tillie glances from the woman to me and back again. "Karen, this is Isaiah. He's the new president of the Brotherhood and a very good friend. Isaiah, Karen is the Intake Coordinator here at the shelter. Without her, this place wouldn't run as smoothly as it does."

I shake Karen's hand and try to recall what Tillie said her title is. When Tillie introduced me as her 'very good friend', my brain didn't process any of the words after that. I latch onto the upgrade and mentally cross my fingers that I don't do anything to fuck it up.

"Nice to meet you, Isaiah."

"You too."

"Karen, why don't we go to my office and we can talk?"

Her office?

"Let me refill my coffee and I'll meet you both there." Karen smiles up at me. "Can I get you anything to drink? Coffee? Water?"

"Coffee would be great, thanks."

"Coming right up."

Karen turns and goes down a hallway, disappearing through a doorway. I follow Tillie in the opposite direction. I peruse the photos hanging on the walls, the drawings that were clearly done by children. I stop when I spot a photo of Tillie standing on what appears to be club property. She's surrounded by laughing children and her face is lit up like a Christmas Tree. Or so it seems. I step forward to get a closer look and notice the way her eyes are wide and bright, but her body is tense, coiled tight. She sure as hell was putting on a show.

"That was such a great day."

Tillie's voice curls around me from behind and I look over my shoulder at her. Her arms are crossed over her chest, her head is tilted, and her smile is sad.

"It looks like you were at the club."

She nods. "It was the first Survivor Celebration." She chuckles as she remembers. "I begged your dad to let me invite the families that were living in the shelter at the time to the club for a huge picnic. It was a year after we opened, and I'd seen so many women and children come through these doors and very few of them had anything to smile about. Or so they thought."

"What do you mean?" I ask as I turn around and lean back against the wall.

"Each and every one of them had a tragic story, an abuser who stole their joy and robbed them of positive experiences. But I saw the flip side of that and needed them to see it too. They were all survivors of their circumstances. Their life experiences up until that point didn't need to define the rest of their lives. I wanted them to have fun and just forget all the bad for a while."

"So, you organized a Survivor Celebration." I can't mask the awe in my voice, the pride in this woman who was clearly broken herself but still made sure others didn't feel that way.

"It didn't take long for your dad to cave. He had a ton of reasons why he didn't think it was a good idea. It could bring trouble to the club's door, the abusers could track the families if they weren't at the shelter, blah blah blah." She waves her hand dismissively. "Then I showed him a picture of Timmy. Two pictures actually. The first was the one that was taken at intake. Timmy was malnourished, dirty, and covered in bruises. The second was a picture that was taken after he'd been here with his mom and little sister for three months. Timmy was sitting in the library we have here and reading a book to his sister. He was smiling, clean, wearing clothes that fit. The change was incredible. Your dad took one look at those pictures and said 'Fuck it. Invite them all. We'll figure out security.'"

"Sounds like Pops."

"Anyway, that year," she nods at the picture on the wall. "We had fifteen families attend. Each in different stages of the process, each with their own stories. Other than the abuse, the one thing they all had in common was having made the decision to get out, get help, make a better life." Tillie takes a deep breath and starts walking down the hall, forcing me to follow. "For as much as your dad balked at the idea, once he was on board, there was no stopping him. That first year, we had so much food we had leftovers for a week, a bouncy house for the kids, a few carnival rides. It was a blast."

"You said it was the first year. Have you had more of these celebrations?"

"We have one every year," she responds proudly. "Each year it gets bigger. Not necessarily because we have more current families, but we invite every family that's ever been here. It's good for those that are in the thick of things to see the success stories. And it's something fun for the kids. They've seen enough shit in their lives. They deserve some happiness. They all do."

I reach out and grab Tillie's hand to whirl her around to

face me. "You are incredible." Her forehead scrunches up and I want to smooth the wrinkles with my thumb. I resist the urge and instead, bend a little so I'm eye level with her. "You might not see it, but I do. Hell, no doubt everyone that's ever stepped foot in this building sees it."

"I'm not though," she argues, although there's no heat behind the words. Only a sad acceptance. "I just know what they've been through."

Tillie tugs her hand free and continues down the hall. With no other choice, but to follow, I do. She may not see what I see but she will. I'll make sure of it.

Tillie stops at a door and punches in a code on the panel on the wall. The sign on the door says 'Director' and for what feels like the hundredth time since I've been home, shock settles in.

"Wait," I say as I cover her hand over the panel. "You're the Director?"

Heat infuses her cheeks and the rosy proof of embarrassment is not a look I'm used to seeing on her. "I'm a co-director."

"That's all you're gonna give me? C'mon, Til," I prod when she offers up no more information.

She heaves a sigh. Before she responds, she punches in a code again and opens the door. She makes her way to the plush chair behind an extremely organized desk. She sits down and opens and closes her mouth several times before she finally speaks. "When you left, it broke me." She presses a tightly clenched fist against her chest. "I was lost, and I felt like my heart had been broken into millions of tiny pieces that would never fit together again."

"I'm so sorry, Til. If I'd—"

"Don't you dare tell me that you would have done things differently or that you wouldn't have left," she snaps. "Don't fucking lie to me, Isaiah."

"Okay."

"Anyway, that first year, I went a little off the rails. Drank too much, partied too hard, did some things I'm not proud of." She inhales deeply and her cheeks puff out as she forces the air back out of her lungs. "After a while, the club had, I don't know, an intervention, I guess. Our moms and Brie kinda took me under their wings. More than normal." She shrugs as if it doesn't matter. "It was an eye-opener. I knew what the club did, about the people they helped. It's not like we were shielded from it growing up. But it was different somehow. I began to see how much evil there really is beyond the walls of BRB property, how much sadness."

My mind reels with thoughts of what she'd seen. I'd seen my fair share of evil and the thought of it coming anywhere near her sits like a lead weight in my gut.

"It was like a switch was flipped. I started school, took as many classes as I could, and worked my way through law school. It was pretty clear early on in my education that I wanted to do more than fight battles in court. I *needed* to do more. So, I partnered with a woman I'd met through some volunteer work and we opened the shelter. Jesse runs the day to day things, and I handle the legal side of it all. She and her husband have a newborn so I'm here a little more now."

"You make it all sound so simple." I lock eyes with her and try like hell not to drown in the swirling blue irises. "What you've built here... Til, it's amazing."

"It's nothing more than what we grew up—"

"Don't let her fool you one little bit." I whirl around at the sound of Karen's voice. She hands me a steaming mug of coffee and sits in the chair next to me, across the desk from Tillie. "Tillie has done amazing things for not only this community but for so many country-wide."

Intrigued, I ask, "How so?"

"Now is not the time," Tillie inserts. "We need to discuss

Susie and the kids." She raises her brows at Karen as if to assert some authority, but it doesn't work.

"And we will," Karen promises but maintains her focus on me. "We get referrals from all over the place. Tillie and Jesse have been asked to speak at conferences, provide training to those opening domestic violence shelters. I know it doesn't look like much from the outside but, Phoenix Rising has the capacity to house up to eighteen families at a time, a library, an in house teacher to provide schooling to the children, a gym, an indoor pool, a large great room, a panic room in case there's a security breach by an abuser, a state of the art security system, office space for all twenty-two staff members, in house legal services, three therapists on staff, a doctor and two nurse practitioners, a computer lab and a commercial kitchen and full-time chef. There is no other shelter that even comes close to providing what we do. And it can all be attributed to Tillie and her vision."

"And now I have a vision of discussing the latest issue with Susie and Mark," Tillie says with a bite in her tone.

Still trying to process everything I just learned, I listen with half an ear as Tillie and Karen shift the conversation to their client. I know Tillie doesn't want to talk about any of the things she's accomplished. She's always been humble, and it seems that hasn't changed but we will talk about it. I may have discovered a lot in the last half hour, but I have a feeling there's so much more.

"... Susie really wants you to sit down with Chad and Carrie. They're having a hard time adjusting without their dad."

"Isn't the dad abusive?" I ask, unable to wrap my brain around the kids not being happy to be safe.

"You have no idea," Karen replies. "But Susie hid it well. She never wanted the kids to know what was going on and until this last time, they didn't. Mark—that's Susie's husband —he beat her so bad that she wasn't able to clean up all the blood before the kids got off the school bus. By then, Mark had passed out drunk and Susie just loaded the twins and Curt, her infant, into the car and went to the police station. They arrived here that evening, and Susie was treated by our physician. Chad and Carrie still don't know the whole story. They're nine and Susie doesn't know what to tell them."

"I'll help with that," Tillie states. "What time is their last class today?"

"Two. That's around the same time that Susie puts Curt down for a nap, so it'll be a good time."

"Where is Mark now?" I ask.

"He sat in jail for a few weeks but then his lawyer got him out on bail. The prosecutor's office is working on preparing their case for attempted murder. The judge did order Mark to wear an ankle monitor and by all accounts, he's doing that, but I'm concerned that he'll find a way around it."

"Has a prosecutor been assigned yet?" Tillie leans forward and braces her elbows on the desk.

Karen's eyes narrow in confusion. "Yeah, it's Henry. He didn't tell you?"

"Jesus, he's like a piece of gum stuck to the bottom of your shoe." I try to inject some levity into my tone but fail miserably. The last thing Tillie needs is more time with Henry. Shit, it's the last thing *I* need.

Karen looks from Tillie to me and back again. "What's going on?"

"Henry and I broke up." Karen's face registers her shock and when she opens her mouth to speak, Tillie holds up her hand. "I don't want to talk about it."

Karen nods but she doesn't look very happy about not being told the juicy details. I don't know Karen that well and

I certainly haven't witnessed much interaction between her and Tillie, but they seem like they're close. Is Tillie not talking to her because I'm here? Or is there some other reason?

"Let Susie know that I'll sit down with her and the twins after she puts Curt down for his nap. I'll be around all day so she can come and find me or have someone page me over the intercom."

"I'll let her know," Karen assures her and then glances at her watch. "I've got an intake in an hour. A woman and her four-year-old daughter. She's being driven here by our liaison in Tennessee."

I watch Tillie's reaction to the child's age. Most people wouldn't be able to see the pain that flashes in her eyes, but I do. I know her story. I know her. She shakes her head, almost imperceptibly, and her chest rises and falls with her deep breaths.

"I'll make sure a suite is ready for them." Tillie flattens her palms on the surface of her desk and stands. "Anything else?"

Karen stands as well so I do the same. "Nothing right now. Our liaison says the little girl likes apple juice and peanut butter sandwiches. And her favorite color is purple and she loves picture books."

"Got it."

Curious about this exchange, I watch as Tillie writes the details down on a small notepad and sticks the paper in her pocket. When Karen leaves, silence hangs in the air for what feels like forever but in reality, is only a few seconds.

"Now what?"

"Now," Tillie starts. "We go make sure there's a lot of purple in the suite and stock the mini-fridge with apple juice and the cupboards with bread and peanut butter… among other essentials. Oh, and books. We raid the library for picture books."

"Of course."

And for the first time in probably forever, I let Tillie boss me around with absolutely no ulterior motive other than to make a little girl happy and a mother feel safe.

"Just tell me what to do."

16

TILLIE

"Is that a typical day?"

I look up from my plate and stare at Isaiah across my kitchen table. We didn't get home until seven and we just sat down to eat dinner. The day had been full of things to do and the time passed quickly but now it seems to have slowed down to a crawl.

"Not really," I say after swallowing the mouthful of pizza I'd just put in my mouth. "We don't have intakes every day, but we had a suite open up last week. When I'm there, I typically meet with each resident to go over their legal options and to check in on their progress. It's pretty boring but I love it."

"I could tell. You seemed to really enjoy getting everything ready with the suite. And the look on that little girl's face when she saw the giant purple stuffed unicorn on her bed was priceless."

I laugh as I remember the way her eyes lit up and she ran excitedly to jump on the bed and give 'sparkles' a hug. Sobering a little, I lock eyes with Isaiah. "Thank you, by the way. You didn't have to buy that thing for her."

"Oh, come on," he taunts. "I had fun shopping for her. Besides, I've got money saved up, and what better way to spend it than on a child's happiness?"

"Most people could think of a lot of things."

"I'm not most people." He smirks and I can't help the grin that spreads across my own face.

"No, Isaiah, you certainly aren't most people."

The rest of the meal is eaten in silence and when we're done, Isaiah cleans up our dishes and takes out the trash. I watch him do these things, even offer to help, but he insists that I 'sit down and relax'.

No need to tell me twice. My body is still sore from my attack and I'm exhausted. I turn on the TV and switch it to Netflix. I pull up my favorite show and hit play on episode one. My eyelids are heavy, and I struggle to keep them open.

When the couch cushion dips, I jolt awake and see Isaiah sitting next to me.

"Come here."

He holds his arms open and I don't even think twice before scooting closer and curling against him. It briefly crosses my mind that this is a bad idea but only briefly. I'm too damn tired to think it to death. Besides, it feels so good to be held by someone, by *him*.

Completely relaxed, I let Isaiah's steady heartbeat and the light graze of his fingertips against my skin lull me to sleep. I have no idea how long I doze but I wake up to the sound of rain pelting the windows mixed with Isaiah's snoring.

The television has the 'are you still watching Netflix' message on it so I must have been out for a while. I slide out from under Isaiah's arm, careful not to wake him. I pull the blanket from the back of the couch and lay it over his sleeping form and start to make my way through the house to turn off all the lights and to set the alarm.

By the time I'm in my own bed, another hour has passed

and any hope of falling back to sleep is gone. I grab my cell phone off of my nightstand and pull up the texting app. It's late but there's one person I can always count on to respond, no matter what.

Me: Can't sleep

It only takes a few seconds for those three little dots to appear. I watch them as if that'll make the response come quicker.

Isabelle: Me 2. Bro still there?

Me: Yep

Isabelle: Then why r u texting me?

Me: He's asleep

Isabelle: Wake him up

That last text is followed by no less than a dozen winking face emojis. I laugh at her antics. Only Isabelle would be trying to get me, and her brother, laid.

Me: Not happening

Isabelle: Oh yeah?

As I'm typing a response, I hear a phone ring in another part of the house, and then Isaiah's deep, gritty, sexy as fuck voice reaches me. Oh shit.

Me: You didn't?!?!?

It's another few minutes before those dots appear and by then, Isaiah is no longer talking, and I can hear footsteps on the stairs.

Isabelle: Have fun!

I toss my phone on the bed beside me and roll over to groan into my pillow. I make a mental note to kick Isabelle's ass the next time I see her.

"Til?" Isaiah's voice drifts through the door after he knocks softly. "You awake?"

I roll my eyes because he knows I'm awake. His blabbermouth sister already told him that. The question is, what else did she tell him to get him to come up here.

"Yeah, I'm awake."

The door swings open and Isaiah steps through. It's hard to see him with only the moonlight illuminating the room but I don't need to see him to picture exactly what he looks like.

"Is everything okay?" He sounds tired, almost as tired as I felt earlier.

"That depends." I toss the blanket off of me and get up from the bed. "What did Isabelle tell you?"

"Just that you couldn't sleep."

"And you came up here, why?"

The floorboards creak beneath his weight as he closes the distance between us. A shiver races down my spine when his hands settle on my arms and he rubs them up and down as if to warm me. Little does he know, I'm not cold. I'm fucking burning hot and he's not helping.

"You seemed to sleep pretty well downstairs. I wanted to see if there was anything I could do to help." There's a teasing quality to his voice, mixed with a tinge of hope.

"And how would you help?"

I slide my arms around his waist and press my cheek to his chest, wishing the entire time that he didn't have a shirt on so we could be skin to skin.

"What do you want me to do?"

"I don't know."

Isaiah takes a step back and separates himself from me. He grips my chin and tips my face up. "Would this work?" he asks in a husky voice.

I have no time to formulate an answer. He dips his head and touches his lips to mine. At first, the kiss is light, tentative, almost as if he's asking for permission.

His tongue darts out and he traces my bottom lip with it, alternating between licking and nibbling. Somehow, my hands make their way to the front of his jeans and I curl my fingers over the waistband. Fuck permission. I want to have to beg for forgiveness.

Isaiah bends and lifts me up with my ass cradled in his large hands. My legs instinctively go around him and I lock my ankles at his back. The kiss deepens, becomes frenzied. He turns and takes the few steps to the wall, where he slams me against it.

With his weight holding me in place, his hands are free to roam and they're everywhere. My face, my hair, under my shirt and cupping my tits. He tugs the cup of my bra down and exposes my nipple with lightning-quick speed. I break the kiss long enough to yank my shirt over my head and put myself on display for him.

Isaiah slows his movements and trails his lips down my chin, down my neck, before sucking my nipple between his lips and swirling his tongue around it. Heat pools between my thighs and my head falls back as a moan escapes me.

"I… this… holy hell."

My words are incoherent but somewhere in the farthest recesses of my brain, I know this is a bad idea. Not because I don't want it. At this moment, I want it more than life itself. But what about tomorrow? What will I want then?

I slowly float back to reality, back to sanity, and press my hands against his shoulders to get him to stop. Immediately, he pulls his head back and stares into my eyes.

"What?"

"This isn't going to help me sleep." Inwardly, I groan. Stupid, so stupid.

"That's because we aren't done." He kisses me again and I almost lose control. When he pulls away, he's grinning like the Cheshire Cat. "You'll sleep like a baby if you give me another hour."

"An hour?" I taunt. "Neither of us would last an hour and you know it."

"Probably not. But that's beside the point." He tilts his head. "Wait. What exactly is the point again?"

I laugh at him as I swat at his pecs. "Put me down." He releases me and my feet touch the floor. "The point is, this isn't a good idea. At least, not yet."

"Okay."

"Okay? That's it? You're not going to try to convince me otherwise?" I ask incredulously. I was expecting some resistance.

"Nope." Isaiah threads his fingers through mine and tugs me back to the bed. He gently pushes me down and crawls in beside me, pulling the blanket over us both.

"What are you doing?"

"Helping you sleep. Generally, you have to close your eyes for that to happen."

I sigh, feigning frustration, but inside, one of the misfit pieces of my heart slides back into its rightful place. I roll over so my back is to him and he wraps an arm around my stomach.

"G'night, Til."

"Night."

Several minutes pass before his breathing seems to even out and I think he's asleep. Only then do I allow myself to close my eyes and savor the feel of him. Right before I fall over that edge of consciousness, I hear something that causes another misfit piece to slide into its rightful place.

"I love you, Til."

17

ISAIAH

"I know that look."

I glance up from the desk in the library at the main house and see Isabelle standing in the doorway with a smug look on her face. I shake my head at her but otherwise, I try to ignore her.

"Jace still good with the Sloops?" I ask Liam, who's sitting across from me.

"You can't ignore me forever, brother," Isabelle chuckles.

"I can try," I say, hoping she takes the hint.

"You can also try to lasso the moon. Not ever gonna happen."

"What do you want from me, Iz?" I drop the papers in my hands onto the desk and lean back in my chair. "You wanna hear that your plan worked? Or would you like to hear how it left me with a severe case of blue balls?" I raise one eyebrow, daring her to keep pushing.

Liam gives me a questioning look but wisely keeps his mouth shut.

"Point made," Isabelle pouts. She straightens and a bright smile appears. "I'll just talk to Tillie."

"Leave Tillie alone, Iz," I demand. "I'm serious. Let us figure out our own shit."

"Do you really think that she's gonna keep details from me? C'mon, Isaiah, even you aren't that dumb."

"Girl's got a point," Liam adds his two cents.

"Shut up."

"Shut it."

Isabelle and I snap simultaneously, and Liam holds his hands up in mock surrender.

"Fine. I'm leaving."

She turns around to leave but the little demon on my shoulder gets the best of me.

"Izzy?"

"Yeah?" she asks looking over her shoulder.

"Tell me everything later."

"You got it." With those parting words, she winks and then disappears down the hallway.

"I don't think I'll ever get used to your weird relationship with each other." Liam shakes his head.

"It's a twin thing."

Most people don't understand mine and Isabelle's relationship, our sibling bond. I always give the same 'it's a twin thing' reasoning and am generally met with disbelieving looks. Unless you're a twin, you'll never understand. Isabelle and I fought like cats and dogs growing up, but I was always the first in line to knock sense into anyone that hurt her or looked at her wrong. That hasn't changed just because we're adults.

"Back to business," I prompt. "Jace and the Sloops?"

"I'm pretty sure that case will wrap up soon. Good ol' Daryl got picked up for assault with a deadly weapon the other night and according to the sheriff, he'll be serving a decent amount of time between that and all of his priors." Liam's grin matches my own. We live for this shit, for assholes getting what's coming to them. "Jace got Rachel set up with some new documentation and is taking her to a new location tomorrow. He's not happy about it because he likes her, but he knows it's the job. He'll be back from that run the day after tomorrow."

"Good." I glance at my laptop. "What about Noah and Adam? What are they up to?"

"Both are free for new clients. We don't really have much on our plate right now." Liam picks his cell up and scrolls through it, for what, I don't know. "We're gonna have to start planning this year's Survivor Celebration. That's in a few months and Tillie runs a tight ship when it comes to anything related to the shelter."

"She told me about that. But she didn't tell me when it was exactly."

"Doesn't surprise me."

"Why?"

Liam breaks eye contact and looks toward the window as if trying to choose his words carefully. When he looks back at me, his expression is somber.

"Isaiah, man, I love you. You've been more like a brother to me than a friend. And I would lay my life on the line for you. But what you did?" Anger seeps into his expression. "It was fucked up. When she came back from your graduation, she was a shell. A damn shell full of bitterness and hatred and pain and… shit, I don't know. Every bad thing you can think of."

Liam shoots up from his chair and starts to pace. I follow his movement but say nothing.

"Do you have any idea how many nights Iz, me, or Lila had to go pick her up from some bar because she was too fucking drunk to stand up, let alone drive? Or how many times the three of us would sit up and pray that when our phones rang it was just a bartender calling to say she needed that ride and not the cops?"

"I didn't know." The excuse is weak but it's all I've got.

"Of course, you didn't!" He shouts, his rage increasing with each passing second. "Not only were we all trying to live our own lives and process what happened, but we also had the club. Aiden and Scarlett fought so much over how to handle Tillie. Did you know that? Did you know that they almost got divorced?"

I shake my head. Of course, I didn't know. I'd have come home if I had.

No, you wouldn't have. It wouldn't have changed anything.

"No one told me."

"Are you serious?" Liam stops at the edge of the desk and leans his weight on his palms and gets within inches of my face. "Tillie wrote you so many goddamn letters and you never once responded. Your parents called so many times and were always told that you couldn't be reached because you were on some mission. Well, *Prez*," he snarls. "I've got news for you. You managed to save everyone else while simultaneously destroying the very people you should have concerned yourself with."

My heart pounds behind my ribs and my ears ring. Liam is so close, and his fury is fueling my own. "You better back the fuck up," I growl, rising from my chair and matching his stance.

"Or what?"

"Liam, either calm the fuck down, back the fuck up, or get the fuck out." My tone is laced with steel and full of warning.

"No, I'm not going to do any of those things. Ya know why?" When I remain silent and stone-faced, he continues. "Because I don't run." I straighten to my full height but he doesn't back down. "I don't know what shit you went through over there, but it's clear that I'm triggering you.

Maybe someday you'll trust me enough to tell me. But for now, if no one else is gonna call you on all the bullshit or be honest with you about how things went down after you left then I guess it's up to me to do it. Seems only fair since I'm your VP. And if that means you pummel me, then so fucking be it."

Pain spreads through my fingers and up to my wrist as my hand connects with his jaw. Liam's head rears back and he cups his nose to catch the blood but only for a second. He drops his hands to his sides and straightens his shoulders.

"Go ahead, hit me again," he taunts, blood oozing from his nose and dripping onto the hardwood floor.

I throw a right hook, catching his cheek and I hear the bone crack.

"Is that all you got?" Still, he remains straight, unmoving.

I throw a few more punches, alternating between my left and right fists, spreading out the pain. And the entire time I'm lashing out, Liam stands there and takes hit after hit after hit. It doesn't take long before my arms tire out although I don't think it's physical exhaustion. My emotions just catch up to me and slow me down.

I drop to the floor and hang my head in my hands, unconcerned about my own blood and smearing it on my face and in my hair. My eyes burn but I do nothing to stop the tears that well up. Liam sits next to me and puts his arm around my shoulders and holds me like only a brother, only someone who loves you could do.

I don't know how long we sit there, both of us bloody, both of us reeling from what happened. At some point, he claps me on the back and stands up, reaching his hand down to help me. I clasp his hand and let him pull me off the floor.

"Feel better?" he asks.

"A little." I take in the damage to his face. "Damn, I'm sorry, man."

"Don't sweat it. Apparently, we both had to let some shit out today."

I nod and just like that, it's forgotten. I have no illusions that it'll never be brought up or that I won't have to answer for all the things he told me. But for now, we're okay.

We walk out of the library and into the main room to grab a few beers. As soon as I reach the middle of the room, my dad walks through the door, takes one look at us, and stops in his tracks.

"Jesus Christ. What the fuck happened?" He directs his question to Liam, likely because his face is the one that's sporting more damage.

Liam shrugs. "Ran into a door." He glances at me. "Several times."

My dad looks from Liam to me to Liam and then settles his gaze on me. "Are *you* okay?"

That isn't what I was expecting at all. I thought for sure he'd rip me a new one. My shoulders sag when he doesn't, and I breathe a sigh of relief.

"Yeah. I'm okay. At least, I will be."

He gives a tight nod. "Good. Glad to hear it. Now," he tips his head toward the door. "Go see Doc and let him check you both over."

"We're fine, Pops," I argue like a petulant child.

"Go. Now." The authority in his voice is so reminiscent of my childhood that I can't help but grin. "I may not be your president but I'm still your dad. And I can't still kick your ass." He eyes me up and down. "Especially now."

I heave a sigh but Liam and I both make our way out of the main house. Once we clear the porch, we both bust up laughing, at what, I don't know. But it feels good. Hurts like a son of a bitch after that fight but it feels right.

It feels like one more step towards actually being home.

18

TILLIE

"What are you so worried about? You never take this much time to get ready."

I meet Isabelle's stare in the mirror. It's Sunday and that means we've got 'family' dinner at the main house. Normally, I'd throw on whatever is clean but this week is different. This week, Isaiah will be there. It's the first one he's been able to attend since coming home and butterflies are waging war against each other in my stomach.

All I do in response is smirk. She knows exactly why I'm primping. No need to fuel her meddling and give her more ammunition to work with.

"I still can't believe Isaiah beat the shit out of Liam. Have you seen his face?" she asks. "His nose is more crooked than it already was, and I swear it's gonna be different shades of purple for the rest of this life."

Isaiah had told me about the fight. He didn't go into too much detail other than to assure me that whatever had caused it was over and it wouldn't happen again. Of course, I asked Liam for information and he continues to stick to the whole 'I ran into a door' story.

"He'll be fine. Doc said it just might take a few weeks."

I finish with my makeup and give my curls one last spritz of hairspray. If we were riding our bikes to the main house, I wouldn't bother but Isabelle and I decided we'd walk. It's a beautiful day and we intend to enjoy it.

"How do I look?"

I turn to her and hold my arms out. She takes me in from head to toe. I'm wearing a long-sleeved Harley tee that I cut at the neck so that my cleavage spills out and the tightest jeans I own. My boots come almost up to my knees and hug my calves perfectly.

"You look like my dad isn't going to be the only one with heart problems." The sarcasm in her tone doesn't concern me, especially when she laughs and winks to top off her statement.

"Perfect."

I grab my cell phone off of the counter and we head downstairs so we can leave. The walk to the main house goes by quicker than I would have liked and the closer we get, the harder the butterflies fight.

Isaiah's Harley is parked in front of the porch, along with eight others. It's a sight that I will never tire of seeing. Isabelle links her arm in mine and, just like we did when we were teenagers, we walk inside, arm in arm, cackling at our stupidity and childlike behavior.

"It's about…" Isaiah looks over his shoulder from his position on the couch and his eyes seem to bug out of his skull. "Hot damn."

"Told ya." Isabelle nudges me.

Isaiah stands and walks around the sofa, only stopping when the toes of his boots are almost touching mine. His cups my cheeks and presses a kiss to my lips, completely ignoring the fact that everyone else is still in the room. It takes him two seconds to make me forget, too.

He breaks the kiss but doesn't pull away. "You look like a heart attack in the making, in the best possible way," Isaiah whispers in my ear seductively.

Even though his kiss, his words, his *voice,* have me vibrating with need, I can't stop the laugh that bursts from my mouth.

"Not the reaction I was hoping for."

He steps back and looks at me with concern. He glances at Isabelle, who has joined in on my laughter.

"What?"

"Oh, brother, she's laughing because that's almost exactly what I said to her."

"You two... you're so much alike it's creepy sometimes," I say when I'm able to catch my breath.

"If you guys are done, dinner's ready."

I stand on my tiptoes to look over Micah's shoulder and see my dad standing across the room with his feet braced apart and his arms crossed over his chest. Even in his sixties, he's an imposing man. But I know him and no doubt, beneath the gruff posturing, he's happy that his Peanut is happy.

Holy shit! I am. I'm happy. When the hell did that happen?

"Good. I'm starving."

I step around Isaiah who just stands there, adjusting himself several times. Nice to know I'm not the only one who's going to struggle through this dinner.

Isaiah finally joins us in the large dining room and conveniently, the only empty chair is next to me. He sits and scoots his chair closer so his knee is touching mine, sending electricity buzzing through my system.

Under the table, I place my hand on his thigh and slowly slide it up until it's resting on his junk and then give a little squeeze. Two can play at this game.

He leans down and puts his lips next to my ear and whispers, "You're gonna pay for this."

"We'll see." I bat my lashes at him and give him my best saucy smile.

He shakes his head and chuckles. The next few minutes are a blur of sizzling, sneaky touches as everyone fills their plates. Just as I stab a piece of chicken with my fork and bring it to my mouth, my cell phone vibrates in my pocket. I take the bite and then pull my phone out to look at it.

When I read the text, I stand up so fast that my chair crashes to the floor behind me, echoing against the hardwood. "I gotta go."

I race to the front door and pull it open, only to have it slammed shut with a hand from behind me.

"What the hell, Til? What happened?"

Isaiah braces himself on his outstretched arm and it's clear that he's not going to let me go without an explanation. And for once, I don't want to argue. I may need his help. I may be independent and perfectly capable of handling myself, but I'm not stupid.

"Karen texted me our danger word."

"Danger word?" He arches a brow.

"Yeah, ya know, kinda like a safe word but for danger." I'm talking so fast that I force myself to slow down so I can make him understand. And having to do that pisses me off because I don't have time to waste. "We've got our alarm system at the shelter and it goes off if there's a breach in security. But just in case..." I sigh dramatically, realizing that I'm doing exactly what I don't have time for. "C'mon. We'll take the Jeep and I'll explain on the way."

I manage to strong-arm him away from the door and yank it open. I rush to the Jeep and climb in behind the wheel. I throw the vehicle in drive just as Isaiah gets his leg inside and is shutting the door.

"Jesus, slow down."

"No time." I press the gas pedal harder and send dirt and gravel spraying behind us.

"Tell me what the fuck is going on," he demands.

I barrel out onto the main road, whipping the steering wheel so fast that Isaiah latches on to the 'oh shit' handle.

"Right." I toss my phone into his lap. "Pull up Karen's contact info and dial. Put it on speaker. She'll pick up but she won't talk."

He does as I instruct and I'm grateful. Karen does answer the phone after two rings and the sound on the other end is muffled for a moment before it seems to clear up, almost like she took it out of her pocket and set it down somewhere with the speaker pointing up.

"You stupid bitch!" I recognize that voice. "Tell me where the fuck my kids are!"

"Who is that?" Isaiah whispers, having caught on to at least the urgency of the situation and that we need to be as quiet as possible so we don't tip anyone off that Karen answered her phone.

"That," I start and take a deep breath. "Is Mark. Susie's husband." I glance at him quickly. "You remember her from—"

"Yeah. Yeah, I remember." He nods. "If I'm reading this right, Karen and you have a word that you use to text each other if there's a dangerous situation. If for some reason the alarm system doesn't work and if calling the cops isn't necessarily the best option."

"Yes."

"Does this mean that Mark is at the shelter? Is that where this is going down?"

"Yes."

"Fuck!"

"Exactly." I navigate the turn onto the dirt road that the shelter is on and kill the headlights.

"What about the residents? If he's inside, how has he not gotten to them."

"We've got the panic room. There's a hidden button in every room of the shelter that can be pushed so that an alert goes to each resident's cell phone if they're in the building. If they get that alert, there's protocol on how to get to the panic room, based on the room that the alert came from."

"Wow. I'm impressed."

"That's great," I snap, my adrenaline racing, my palms sweating. I'm not mad at him. He just happens to be the only available target for my rage.

"How many times have you had to do this?"

"In the five years we've been open, this makes the fourth time. But every single time, it's like the first time. Each abuser is different, presents different threats." I see Mark's vehicle parked out front with the driver's door thrown open and the interior light on. I drive past him and turn onto a hidden path that leads to the back of the building. "Mark is by far the most dangerous we've had."

When I park the Jeep, I jump out and race toward the corner of the building. Isaiah is on my heels.

"You aren't going in there," he states matter-of-factly.

"Yes, I am." I whirl on him, ready to fight if I have to. "Listen, I know you want to protect me and you're some big bad Navy Seal, but this is my problem. These are my people. This is my fight. I'm glad you're here and I'm smart enough to know I could use your help but if you think this is your show to run then you can go sit your fucking ass in the car and wait."

I yank out of his hold and turn back to the brick. It's hard to see, but there's one brick that has a small imprint of a Phoenix on it. That is the only spot on the outside of the building that gives any indication of what this place is. I press my thumb into the Phoenix and the surrounding bricks pop and shift to open a door.

I grin over my shoulder at Isaiah and see his eyes grow round.

"This is some spy level shit. Maybe you should be president of the club."

"Maybe I should be."

We make our way inside and I go straight to my office and punch in the code. When I enter, I quickly log into my computer and pull up the security footage. It takes a minute, but I find the camera that is pointing directly at Mark and Karen. Good, she managed to get him near the front of the building. The panic room is at the back, not far from my office, so she's doing great.

The knife at her throat tells a different story though. We can still hear Mark and Karen through my cell phone and Karen's starting to struggle with keeping him engaged in conversation and diverting his attention from his goal.

I check one last location: the panic room. It's full to capacity but it appears that everyone is inside. The residents are doing a great job of keeping the kids occupied and remaining as calm as possible. It also looks like there's a movie playing, which helps to drown out any noise so the kids can't hear what's going on.

I open the bottom drawer of my desk and punch in yet another code. Once the lock disengages, a lid pops up and I reach in to pull out my Glock.

"What the hell are you gonna do with that?"

"What do you think?"

I push past him and make my way down the hallway. I glance over my shoulder and see him holding his own weapon: a Glock that his dad gave him years ago.

"You can't go in that room with me," I inform him, fully expecting an argument.

"Doesn't mean I won't be ready for whatever happens." My shock must register on my face because he clarifies. "I know me going in with you will only set him off more. I do remember everything we were taught."

I nod just as we reach the doorway that leads to the room Karen and Mark are in. Mark is going on and on about how his wife and children belong to him and he has a right to know where they're at. I shove my Glock in my waistband at the back of my jeans and pull my shirt out over it.

"I will ask one more goddamn time," Mark grits out and waves his hands around maniacally. "Where are my wife and kids?"

"Mark?"

I step through the doorway and keep my voice even. Still, the sounds cause him to whirl around and I lock eyes with him, forcing myself to not look at Karen because if I do, I'll probably lose my shit.

Mark advances on me and I make sure to keep my hands up in front of me so he doesn't view me as a threat. He stops about a foot in front of me. His chest is heaving, his face red with rage and his hands are clenched into fists at his sides. I take in his swollen knuckles and the drying blood on them.

"Mark, I'd like to help you. I really would, but first, you're going to need to calm down."

"Calm down?" Ironically, his voice is deathly calm now, but his body language is projecting anything but. "You dumb cunt! I'll calm down when I'm walking out of here with my family."

The scent of booze wafts up my nostrils. That combined with Mark's bloodshot eyes, and I know he's drunk. That makes him even more dangerous and unpredictable.

"That's going to be hard to do because they aren't here,

Mark. No matter what you do to Karen or me, you can't leave here with Susie and the kids." I refuse to call them his family. He lost the right to have them labeled as that the second he laid a hand on Susie.

"Liar!" He yells and spittle flies from his mouth. He begins to pace. "I know they're here. Susie's brainless sister caved." When he retraces his steps and I can see his face, the evil smile I see scares me. "Ya know what that bitch did?"

"No, I don't know what she did." I also don't recall Susie having a sister, but now isn't the time to try to remember what's written in a file.

"She made the mistake of thinking I wouldn't hurt her." The way he laughs at that reminds me of a hungry hyena. "I'm pretty sure her broken arm has taught her a very valuable lesson. Don't fuck with me."

My muscles tense and the professional in me reminds the enraged part of me that I need to let him keep talking. Everything he says is being recorded and will be given to the cops as evidence to use against him. Then the enraged part of me reminds the professional part that Mark is related to a few of the cops in this county. He's also the son of the former Governor, which is why he's not already behind bars and why, when he is arrested, he always gets out.

Motherfucker!

I shake my head to clear my thoughts and refocus on the current situation. "I don't want to fuck with you." I take a step toward him to gage how he reacts. His eye twitches, but that's the only indication that my movement affected him at all. "I want to see you reunite with Susie and the kids. They need their father." The words pass my lips and I have to swallow the bile that threatens at the lie.

"That's right," he says, with less heat in his tone. He glances over his shoulder at Karen. "See, she gets it."

"I do. I do get it." I take another step forward.

"So, you'll go get them, bring them to me?"

I shake my head. "I can't. They aren't here."

In an instant, Mark has his fist wrapped around a fistful of my hair and is yanking so hard my scalp burns. His face is so close to mine that I feel his hot breath skate across my cheek, and I think I can hear his heartbeat.

"Listen bitch," he snarls. "I don't give a shit where they are. Even if they aren't here, you know how to get a hold of them. I suggest you do that." He tilts his head. "Unless you *want* to die."

The gunshot startles Mark enough that he loosens his grip on me. I'm able to put some distance between us but before I can blink, Isaiah is next to me. I guess I should be thankful that he waited this long to interfere. Judging by the look on his face and the eerie calm he's projecting, it was hard for him to stand back as long as he did.

"Call her a bitch one more time you stupid fuck." Isaiah's tone is laced with steel. "I dare you." Mark remains silent. "The next time you threaten someone, you better be damn sure that there isn't any way else around." He lifts his gun up as if to show it off. "Especially someone with a gun."

"You won't shoot me," Mark taunts.

"Care to test that theory?"

Mark's reaction would be comical under other circumstances. He's your everyday run of the mill bully. He has no problem going up against people his own size or smaller but put him in front of a 6'4" wall of solid muscle and he backs off.

"You've got one week," Mark informs me. "I want my family at my front door, begging me to take them back within the week."

Mark returns to Karen's side and wraps his fingers around the back of her neck. Karen's eyes widen but she shakes her head almost imperceptibly. He's not hurting her too badly but rather trying to prove a point.

"If they aren't there when your time is up, I'll come back and gut this bitch." He drops his arms and walks backward towards the only visible entrance of the building. Just before he shoves through the door, he calmly continues. "And then I'll hunt you down and wait until you're alone to make you suffer."

He whirls around and disappears through the door and around the corner where his vehicle was haphazardly parked. I release the pent-up breath I was holding and rush to Karen.

"Are you okay?"

"A little shaken up," she replies. "Nothing a few shots of Bourbon can't cure."

"I think I'll join you for that drink after we check on everyone."

A large hand settles on my back and I glance up and see Isaiah standing next to me. "We need to call the police."

"I will. Not that they'll do anything." I turn to face him. "He's related to half the important people in the state. He'll get arrested but he won't stay put for long. He never does."

"Hopefully he'll stay long enough to get Susie and the kids to another location. They can't stay here now."

"She won't leave." I explain to him how I'd tried, several times, to convince her to relocate. "She says she refuses to let him control any more of her life than he already has." I shrug. "On one hand, I'm proud of her and on the other, I want to knock some sense into her. But it's her choice, not mine. And we'll support her in any way we can, whether we agree or not."

Isaiah doesn't argue. Like me, he may not agree, but he's been around enough domestic violence to know I'm right.

"Karen, can you call the police and report everything?

Isaiah and I will go check on everyone. You can use the phone in my office. We'll meet you there once they're all settled."

"You got it."

Karen retreats down the hallway Isaiah and I came through when we arrived. The moment she's out of sight, Isaiah wraps his hand around the back of my head and pulls me toward him, pressing his lips to mine.

I slant my head to accommodate the kiss. It doesn't last long but it's enough to make me want more, so much more.

"Please don't ever ask me to do that again," he says as he leans his forehead against mine.

"What?"

"Stand back and watch a man lay his hands on you, threaten you."

"I can handle myself. I appreciate that you care, Isaiah." I lace my fingers with his. "I really do. But I've been taking care of myself for a long time now and that's not going to change."

"I know you can. I'm not asking you to give up your independence, Til. I'd never take that from you." He brushes a stray curl behind my ear. "But this is who I am. I never want to see you hurt. Hell, I never want to be the one to hurt you. Not again. I know you said you need time and that's fine, but I protect what's mine."

I arch a brow. "Now you're claiming me? Outright?"

Isaiah grins, displaying a dimple in his left cheek and even white teeth.

"Damn straight." His smile slips for a second and he says, "You never did tell me what the danger word is."

Now, I'm the one grinning.

"Blowjob. The danger word is blowjob."

19

ISAIAH

"Well, shit."

I shift my gaze to Tillie. After ensuring that everything was fine after the incident with Mark at the shelter, she agreed to let me drive us home. She's been silent the entire ride but now she's looking at her phone and she does not look happy.

"What?"

She turns her phone so I get a quick glance at the screen. She doesn't leave it up long enough for me to determine anything other than she must have gotten a text.

"Henry just texted me asking when I was going to come to his office to go over the case against the Uber driver."

"I thought we made it pretty clear that we'd schedule that through his office."

"We did." Tillie slaps her phone against her thigh. "Dammit! Why can't he just slink away like you did?"

I navigate the turn onto club property and hit the brakes, throwing the Jeep into park. Twisting in my seat, I glare at her. She glances at me and seems surprised at my obvious anger.

"What?" she prods.

"What?" I repeat. "What do you mean 'what'? I didn't fucking slink off, Til. I joined the military. There's a big difference."

She sighs dramatically. "Do you really want to do this now?"

"No, I don't, but I think we have to." What I don't say is I don't ever want to do this, fight with her. Especially about things that we can't change. "You're holding a grudge the size of the fucking Grand Canyon and I don't know how we get past that. Are you ever going to forgive me or are we wasting our time?"

Tillie looks at her phone, but it doesn't appear that she's really seeing what's in front of her. She's avoiding the conversation, hoping that her silence will end it.

Too fucking bad.

When she remains silent, I lean across the center console and grip her chin, forcing her to look at me. She tries to avert her gaze but eventually makes eye contact. Still, she says nothing.

"You really have nothing to say?" I ask, beyond frustrated and struggling to maintain any semblance of composure.

Nothing. Not any reaction, whatsoever. I drop my arm and twist back to put the Jeep in gear. I can feel her eyes on me, making me itch to keep trying to get a reaction from her, but I don't.

When we pull up in front of her house, she doesn't even wait until the vehicle stops before she's climbing out and rushing up the steps. I watch as she unlocks her door and slams it behind her. I don't know if she thinks she can keep me out or what, but a closed door isn't going to stop me. Not when it comes to her.

I pull my own cell out of my pocket and text Aiden to let him know that Tillie is okay. She took off from dinner quickly and there hadn't been time to let anyone know what was going on. He responds quickly, thanking me for 'taking care of her'. I also send a quick text to my dad, giving him the same information. I don't get a response from him, but I will eventually.

I make my way inside and am greeted by silence. Imagine that. I stand just inside the front door for several minutes before I hear the shower turn on. I take a few steps toward the stairs but stop short of actually going up them.

Tillie's voice is in my head, telling me to go to BUD/S training, telling me that she will support me. Bitterness settles in. Bitterness and fury. What the fuck does she want from me? I did exactly what she told me to do eight years ago, yet here we are. I'm being made to pay for listening to her.

What makes it an even harder pill to swallow is that things wouldn't have been any easier if I hadn't listened to her and stayed home. I'd have ended up resenting her. It was a lose-lose situation.

Unable to stand being cooped up in the house, I shove open the door and yank it shut behind me. I make sure to lock it because even though I'm pissed, I want her safe. I jog down the steps and to the main house where Nyx is parked.

The closer I get to my bike, the more enraged I feel. Emotions assault me and by the time I fire Nyx up, I'm itching to go a round with someone, anyone, to get rid of all the pent-up rage I'm carrying around.

I've already taken out my frustrations on Liam so that's out. I do the only other thing I can do, the only other thing that can calm the beast inside. I weave my way through the winding back roads to Elephant Hill where I park and climb to the top to clear my head.

~

Tillie

The slamming door startles me, and I step out of the shower to open the bathroom door. The lock of the front door clicks into place just as I stick my head out.

"That's it! Fucking leave!" I shout, knowing full well Isaiah won't hear me. "Again," I say to myself.

Water drips from my body and I climb back under the spray. I let the hot water wash away my tears but it does nothing to ease my simmering anger. Not just at Isaiah, but at myself too. I slide down the shower wall and draw my knees to my chest and wrap my arms around them.

Why couldn't I answer Isaiah in the car? Why did my mind go blank when there's so much I want to say to him?

You know why.

When I looked at my phone and saw the text from Henry, I also noticed something else: the date. How it snuck up on me like it did is beyond me. Okay, that's not entirely true. With everything that's happened since Isaiah coming home and, well, Isaiah coming home, it just slipped my mind.

No matter. The fact that I forgot doesn't change anything. I'm still going to stick to my yearly ritual. There's no way that I'm going to let anything, or anyone, take that away from me.

I swipe under my eyes and stand back up to finish my shower. Isaiah should be back soon, and I don't want him to know I've been crying. He's seen it before, many times, but I'm a stronger person now and I really don't want to have to explain the reasoning to him.

I wrap the towel around myself and tuck one corner under so it doesn't fall as I brush my teeth and go through my nightly routine of removing the makeup I didn't get in the shower and moisturizing. When that's done, I hang the towel on the bar and rush to my bedroom naked. Isaiah isn't back because the front door hasn't opened again.

I pull on a pair of baggy sweats and a tank top and head downstairs to eat something. As exhausted as I am, it's still not very late and I need to make every effort to stay awake so Isaiah and I can talk when he gets home. There are things I'm not ready to discuss but I can at least apologize for how I reacted in the car.

With a grilled cheese in hand, I flop down on the couch and put Netflix on. I don't even pay attention to what show I push play on, I just need the noise. I nibble at my sandwich and reflect on the events of the day.

Karen had called the cops and we'd been informed that Mark had been picked up for a DUI shortly after he left the shelter so he's currently sitting in a cell at the county jail. The sheriff did come to the shelter to take our statements and to get copies of the video footage and any recordings we had. Mark will be out in no time if history is any indication, but I can't worry about that right now. For tonight, we're all safe.

I snag my cell phone off of the coffee table to check my email. Ten emails in and there's the confirmation that would have reminded me of the date. I sink into the couch cushion and move on to the rest of the messages. I reply to as many as I can without being at my office and shut close the app.

I turn Netflix off and flip through the channels. I settle on reruns of House Hunters on HGTV and stretch out on the sofa. I don't even get through a full episode before I doze off into a fitful sleep.

A noise startles me awake sometime later and I sit up so fast my head spins. Unable to pinpoint exactly what sound I heard, I prowl the house to make sure nothing seems out of place. I glance out the window to see if Isaiah has returned and he hasn't. The Jeep is still where he parked it, but I know he hadn't taken it when he left. I'd have heard the engine.

I flip on the porch light before double-checking the lock. Convinced that I was hearing things a few minutes earlier, I trudge upstairs and crawl into bed. It's just after three in the morning and I need to get some sleep if I'm going to get an early start.

I stare at the ceiling, wondering where Isaiah is. I check my cell several times to make sure I haven't missed a text or phone call from him but there's nothing. I set my alarm for five and spend the next half hour or so tossing and turning. Where the hell is he?

Just text him.

No.

He's a grown man and doesn't have to check in with you.

I roll over and curl into a ball, unable to quiet the thoughts racing in my head. By the time I manage to fall asleep, I've convinced myself that I don't care where Isaiah is and if he's not back by the time I have to leave then I hope it scares the shit out of him wondering where I am.

20

ISAIAH

"What are you doing here?"

Isabelle is sitting on the chair on Tillie's front porch when I pull Nyx into the drive. I woke up at Elephant Hill and I'm cranky as fuck. I've slept in some awful places, but it's been a while and my body hurts. I may only be twenty-six but right now, I feel more like fifty-six.

"I was hoping to catch Tillie, but I missed her."

The frustration in Isabelle's voice sets my teeth on edge. A glance at my cell tells me it's only seven-thirty and that makes the hairs on the back of my neck stand on edge.

"Where is she?"

"Don't know." I can tell by the way she averts her gaze that she's not being honest.

"Dammit, Iz, ya gotta give me more than that," I snap.

I breeze past her and unlock the front door, calling out to Tillie when I enter. I'm met with silence. I search the house for her, or at least a fucking note, but there's no Tillie and no note. When I return to the living room, Isabelle is standing just inside the door with her arms crossed over her chest and an annoyed look on her face.

"I told you, she's not here."

"Is her car here? Her bike? Where would she have gone? She's not a morning per—"

"Isaiah, stop!" Isabelle shouts, interrupting my rapid-fire questions. At my questioning look, she shakes her head. "Do you know what today is?

"Uh, yeah. It's Monday."

"Well, yeah, it is, but…"

She averts her gaze, again, and I feel my temper rising.

"But what?"

"It's the anniversary of your basic training graduation."

"Okay. What's that got to do with Tillie not being here."

Isabelle releases a long, dramatic sigh. "You better sit down."

She steps past me and sits on the couch. I start pacing and she watches me for a minute before losing control.

"Sit the fuck down," she snaps. "I can't talk to you when you're wearing a hole in the floor."

I glare at her a minute, try to outlast her stare, but I fail. I end up sitting but I'm far from still. My insides are a shaking mess of nerves and emotion.

"Was that so hard?"

"As a matter of fact…"

She laughs at me but quickly sobers. It takes several false starts, but she finally spits out the words she's trying to say.

"Every year, on this date, Tillie takes off."

"Where does she go?"

"The first year it happened, we had no clue where she was," she says, not really answering my questions. "Griffin had to track her phone to find out, but it took time. We were all worried because it'd been such a bad year for her and of course, we all initially thought the worst."

"But if he tracked her, you found her. So where was she."

"Yeah, we found her." Isabelle breathes in deeply and

holds it for a few beats before releasing the breath. "She was at the hotel where they stayed on graduation day."

"Why?"

It's a stupid question, I know, but it's hard for me to wrap my mind around what I'm hearing. I simply don't understand why she would go back to the place where we had our last conversation, where she said her world crashed and burned.

"I don't really know. Tillie tells me everything, but she refuses to talk to me, or anyone else, about it. Trust me, I've tried." She looks at me out of the corner of her eye. "Every single year, I ask her the same questions, and every single year, I get the same response: 'Fuck off.'"

"I'm sorry, I'm not following. Every year?"

"She takes off without a word every year. The first few years, Griffin tracked her back to the same hotel. We finally quit tracking her because it became clear she went to the same place each time." Isabelle shrugs. "I guess we just realized that, for whatever reason, it's something she has to do, so we try to respect that."

"How long does she leave for?"

"She always comes back the next day. I've gone to the hotel a few times to confront her, but I never make it to her room. Her bike is always in the parking lot and I sit for a few hours, never making it inside. I want to talk to her. Shit, I want her to talk to me about it, but I never can quite bring myself to go inside. I figure if her bike is there so is she. The next day, when she gets home, it's like the previous twenty-four hours didn't happen."

A knock on the door startles us both. I turn my head in time to see Liam walking in like he owns the place. He doesn't look at me but focuses on Isabelle.

"Damn. She left, didn't she?" he asks.

"Yeah. I was really hoping she wouldn't go this year, with

this dipshit home." She nods her head at me. "I guess it didn't matter."

"Well, she'll be back tomorrow. We'll give her her space like we always do."

"Fuck that," I roar as I shoot to my feet. "I'm not gonna let her wallow in some hotel room."

I stride past Liam and toward Nyx, trying to ignore their pleas for me to stop.

"Isaiah, don't do this," Liam says as he steps in front of my bike. "Just give her the night."

"Do you have any idea how insane you sound right now? One of our own is alone and hurting and you all just let her do it. I don't get it." I shake my head with disgust and turn my head to look at Isabelle. "And you… you're her best friend. You don't sit in the damn parking lot. You go in and demand she let you in."

"Are you serious?" Isabelle shouts. "Don't you think I wanted to? Especially after everything she went through when you left. We were terrified for her, but she's an adult and can make her own choices. She always comes back and she's always fine for the next three hundred and sixty-four days."

"Not good enough, Iz." I blow out a breath. "I'm going to that damn hotel and I'm going to drag her home, kicking and screaming if I have to. And then we're going to talk. A lot. Because I'm tired of the fighting. I'm tired of my past decisions biting me in the ass all the time. I love her and it's about time she fucking recognizes that."

I rev the engine and they both step out of the way. I take off to make the several hour journey to the damn hotel and bring my woman back home. She better be there, where they say she is. And she better have a good fucking explanation as to why she still took off, even with me home.

21

TILLIE

"Ah, Miss Tillie, you made it."

The man behind the counter beams a smile and greets me the same way he has for the last five years. I lean on my elbows and smile back at him.

"Of course, I made it, Marv." I wink. "You know I wouldn't pass up the chance to see you. How are the grandkids?"

"A pain in my ass." He laughs at himself. "They're good though. I just don't remember teenagers being so entitled. My God, they never get off their phones, always on something called a Snap and Chat." He shakes his head.

"It's Snapchat, Marv." Someone clears their throat behind me, and I slowly turn around. "What's the problem?"

"I'm in a bit of a hurry so if you could stop gabbing like a bunch of schoolgirls, I'd appreciate it."

The man pointedly checks his obnoxious gold watch. I look him up and down, taking in everything from his expensive suit to his shiny dress shoes. I roll my eyes. Entitled prick.

"I'm so sorry, sir," Marv rushes to say from behind me.

Ah, Marv, always professional and doing his best to make everyone's stay here as pleasant as possible. Unless it's me. I put a stop to that stuffy bullshit early on and we've been more like friends ever since. "What can I do for you?"

I twist to grab my key card off of the counter and smile at Marv. "I'll talk to you later Marv. Have a good day."

I walk away toward the bank of elevators. I can hear the man still being shitty with Marv but it's not my place to step in. Besides, Marv may seem to be an older man with no backbone, but first impressions can be deceiving. He's a former Army medic and still has the work ethic and strength of a man in his thirties. I learned that the hard way one year when I went to the hotel gym to work out and he was lifting weights.

I get to my room and slip the key card into the slot, opening the door when the tiny green light flashes. I toss my duffel bag on the floor and go straight to the bathroom. I smile when I see the bath bomb sitting on the counter. Marv started leaving these for me several years ago after his daughter went through what he called a 'hippie phase' and began making her own. He said that I'm his favorite guest and he looks forward to our chats when I show up every year.

I drop down on the bed and think about each year that I've come here. Marv has been around since the year of Isaiah's graduation. That's when our friendship started. Back then, he was handling room service and after my confrontation, he'd delivered the burger and a milkshake I'd ordered. He noticed that I'd been crying and although I didn't know him, everything came pouring out of me when he asked what was wrong.

It was easy to talk to Marv. He didn't know me, but he was kind. He listened to me go on about Isaiah, and how he joined the military. He listened to me talk about how scared I was to live a life without the love of my life. And then he told me the story of him and his wife and how they went through a similar thing when he signed up. Marv is like a surrogate father but one who just lets me be me without any judgment or worry or protectiveness. He's just… Marv.

I force myself to get up and grab the complimentary pen and paper. I also raid the mini-bar and snag all of the small bottles of tequila, whiskey, and vodka. Carrying everything in my hands, I head into the bathroom and start to draw a bath, dropping the bath bomb into the water. I strip out of my clothes, tossing them on the floor, and step into the now green water, enjoying the fizz that swirls around me.

In that moment, soaking in the tub and getting a healthy start on my buzz, I ruminate on what I'll write this year. It's different this time. Isaiah is home. I could tell him everything face-to-face, but it would feel wrong to stop doing what's worked so far.

Knowing that I start to write.

Isaiah,

Here I am, in the same place, I've been ever since the day you broke my heart. I wish you were here. But somehow, it's comforting knowing you're back at my place and will be there when I get home tomorrow. That's such a weird thought. For years, I've only had your memory to hold onto and now I've got the real thing. Problem is, I have no idea what to do with it. When you walked out on me… correction, when I told you to go (see, I can admit my part in it all). I really thought you'd be gone for a short time and miss me so much that you'd just have to come home. But that didn't happen. I wrote to you, begged you to find a way to come see me that first year. You didn't come. You didn't even acknowledge the letter. And once again, my heart broke.

I stop writing and gulp down the whiskey. The liquor burns a path to my gut, and I savor the taste, knowing it'll bring me some measure of calm.

Everyone thinks I don't know that they know where I go every year. They forget that I grew up in the club and know exactly what they're capable of. Griffin can track anyone and I know he did that first year. Isabelle thinks I haven't seen her sitting in the parking lot. I may not talk to them about any of this but it's nice to know they care. Especially when I knew you no longer did. But this time is for me. Me and the memory of you. And if I'm going to talk to anyone about it, it's going to be you. At least, after I'm done yelling (haha).

I set the pen and paper on the side of the tub and reach for the bottle of tequila. I down the entire thing, enjoying the way my head swims with the additional alcohol. I stare at my toes poking out of the water and notice the wrinkles. I've been in here for a while, but I'm not done with my letter and I don't get out until I am.

For a while, I thought about you every single day. I thought and I cried and I thought some more. Think, cry, repeat. Day after day, night after night. I'm not proud of how I tried to forget you. But it happened. And I'm a better person for it now. I may have worked my way through the pain but if I said it didn't still hurt like hell, I'd be lying. And I promised myself that, at least in these letters, I'd never lie. So, there you have it. It still hurts. Fucking bad. And even with you back and living in my house, I don't know how to make it stop. I want to. God knows I want to. And there are times that I can convince myself that the pain is gone. I look at you and am able to pretend that you never left, that I never told you to go. And then reality sucks me back. Fucking reality. The sad thing is, I still want you. I still want the life we always talked about. But I don't know that it's even possible. We've both changed. Do you even want that? Want me? I'm scared to tell you all of this because I won't survive you telling me that you don't. I won't survive if you walk away again. I just won't.

A knock at the door pulls me from my writing. I haven't ordered my usual yet, but Marv must have gotten a jump start for me. I call out instructing whoever is at the door to just leave the tray in my room. I listen as the door opens and closes and then gulp back two more bottles of booze.

By the time I finish my letter, my skin is full-on prune and I'm drunk as hell. Just the way it's supposed to be. I stumble around the bathroom, fumbling with the towel. When I can't get it to stay on my body, I give up and let it fall to the floor. I swipe my hand across the mirror to clear the condensation and stare at my reflection. I can see my scar on my thighs, and I run my fingers over them.

The alcohol I've consumed threatens to reappear, so I forget all about the raised flesh. I drop to my knees, but nothing comes up. When the nausea subsides, I stand and splash water on my face. I don't have the energy to try to get dressed again so I pull the bathroom door open and step into the main room, only to stop in my tracks when I see him sitting on the bed.

I blink several times, trying to clear my vision, certain that I'm seeing things in my drunken state. Nope. He's still there and he's staring at me with an intensity that I want to shrink away from.

"Hello, Tillie."

I manage to pull myself together and stomp toward him, wobbling as I go. "What the fuck are you doing here, Isaiah?" My words are slurred, and my mouth is so dry I'd swear I'd shoved a fistful of cotton balls into it.

"I came to bring you home." He narrows his eyes at me. "Are you drunk?"

"As a matter of fact, I am."

I punch my fist in the air as if to make a point and almost topple over.

"Jesus," he says under his breath. "C'mon, let's get you into bed so you can sleep it off. We'll talk when you've sobered up."

He grabs my arm and urges me closer to the bed. I

struggle against him, trying to extricate myself from his grasp but I fail miserably. The only thing I manage to do is trip over my own damn feet and start to fall. His arms go around my waist to catch me and he pulls me to him. His clothes are rough against my skin, a stark contrast to his gentle fingers.

The ridges beneath the fabric of his clothes tease me and a fire rages inside of me, spreading through my body to ignite a lust so powerful I feel as if I'll explode if it's not fed. I run my hands up his torso and stop at his beard. He was clean-shaven when he came home but I like the rugged look on him. It's sexy as hell.

"Tillie," he starts. "What are you doing?"

I tip my head back and try to lock eyes with him. It's impossible because the room keeps spinning but it doesn't stop me from trying. It doesn't help that the room is dark except for a sliver of light coming through the curtains.

"Kiss me," I breathe and what I intend to sound alluring is not even close.

Isaiah bends at the knees and scoops me up before depositing me on the bed. "I'll kiss you when you're sober." He pulls the blanket over me and places a kiss on my forehead. "Get some sleep."

"Not tired." The words are slurred and I'm struggling to keep my eyes open, but I'm determined to fight it.

"Til, go to sleep. Or pass out. Whatever you have to do so we can talk. Because we're going to talk but not like this."

"Asshole," I mumble.

I hear him chuckle but don't remember anything after that because the booze finally wins.

22

ISAIAH

Fucking hell.

When I arrived at the hotel, I was fully prepared to have to grease a few palms to gain entry into Tillie's room. Imagine my surprise when the staff member at the desk—Marv, I think his name is—called me by name before I even had the chance to speak. Apparently, Tillie talks about me… a lot.

I did have to endure a million questions before he gave me a key. He grilled me much like an overprotective father would and as frustrating as it was, it's nice to know Tillie has someone here looking out for her well-being.

I wasn't surprised to see that her room is the same exact one she stayed in all those years ago. That's just like Tillie.

She moans in her sleep as she tosses and turns, twisting the sheet and blanket in the process. Sitting next to her and not touching her is making me itch beneath my skin. I give in to the urge and reach out to graze her arm. When I make contact, she quiets and draws her knees up tight in her sleep.

I watch her sleep, allowing myself to keep my hand on her arm. When she told me to kiss her, I wanted to. More than I wanted her to sober up. But I knew that if I gave in, that'd be one more thing to fight about when she sobers up. Don't get me wrong, we're gonna fight, of that I'm sure, but I'm smart enough to know that our battles are big enough without adding to them.

"No… no, mmm, no."

Tillie has always mumbled in her sleep. I remember when we were teenagers and we'd sneak out to go to some distant corner of the property to make out. We'd inevitably end up falling asleep in the grass and her sleep talking would always wake me up. I used to think it was funny and tease her about it but now it just makes me sad because it reminds me of how many nights I've missed this.

I trace circles on her shoulder with my fingers and when my cock stirs, I pull away. Now is not the time. Tillie starts tossing and turning again and somehow manages to kick herself completely free of the covers. My dick springs to life at the sight of her naked.

When she came out of the bathroom, I didn't have a chance to enjoy the sight of her, to appreciate her body, her curves, her everything. But now, when she's sleeping, I take in every inch of her from her face to her—

What the fuck?

I lean closer, sure I'm imagining things. Nope, I'm not. Rage courses through me, boiling my blood, at the sight of the puckered flesh on her thighs. I touch one line with the tip of a finger and pull back as if burned. Several times I do this, always recoiling. Not because I'm disgusted. I'm not. Nothing about Tillie could ever disgust me. I recoil because I'm enraged and if I keep touching her, I'm afraid she'll somehow sense the fury and wake up.

I count the lines and there are nine of them. Four on her right thigh and five on the left. Where the hell did they come from? Did she do this to herself? Nothing makes sense and the more I try to rationalize what I'm seeing, the more questions I have.

I force my gaze to move past the scars, down her legs, and a grin spreads across my face when I reach her feet. *Much better.* There's a small tattoo across the top of her foot that reads SYOTOS... see you on the other side. I absently rub my own arm, up and down my bicep, where I have the same tattoo. Sure, the color is different and hers has tiny sunflowers on each end of the abbreviation, but the meaning is the same, the sentiment is the same.

I get up off the bed and make my way to the mini-bar. When I pull open the door, I notice that it's empty. Damn. Hoping that she forgot to drink some, I head to the bathroom and see the empty bottles lying on the floor. Next to them is a pen and pad of paper and I bend to pick them up. Recognizing Tillie's handwriting, I carry it to the chair in the main room and flip on the small light so I can read it.

My eyes burn as I scan the words, *her* words. I reread them several times, even more questions swirling in my head. I drop my hand to my lap, maintaining my grip on the paper, and let my head fall back. Well, at least I know she loves me.

"What are you doing?"

I don't move my head when I respond. "What does it look like?"

I don't know why I'm being an ass. I've ridden a roller coaster of emotions today and this letter is just one more curve thrown at me.

"I'm gonna be..."

I hear a thump and raise my head in time to see Tillie run to the bathroom and slam the door. I follow her and hear her retching before I get the door open. I test the knob and push the door open when I find it unlocked. Tillie is on the floor in front of the toilet, her body convulsing as she expels the booze she consumed.

I turn on the cold water and wet a washcloth. Kneeling beside her, I place it on her forehead and pull her hair back out of her face.

"That's it, Til. Get it all out."

"Leave me al—"

Her muscles coil and she can't even finish her sentence before she starts dry heaving. I flush the toilet and when the heaving subsides, I stand to rinse out the washcloth. I kneel back down just as Tillie straightens for a moment before falling back to sit on her ass and not her knees.

"Please, Isaiah," she pleads weakly. "Let me puke in peace."

"Sorry, no can do."

I rub her body with the cold washcloth, and she groans but she doesn't fight me. She doesn't have the energy to. She drops her head and rests it on her arms on her drawn-up knees. Several minutes pass and when she doesn't start puking again, I pick her up in my arms and carry her to the bed.

"Why are you here," she asks as I draw up the sheet to cover her.

"Why do you think I'm here, Til?"

"I don't know. Because your sister has a big fucking mouth and you decided to be as annoying as possible."

I chuckle at her smart mouth. At least if she's copping an attitude, I know she's feeling a little better.

"Before I answer your question, I've got several of my own."

"That's not how this works. We're not playing twenty questions."

"Yeah, Til, we are. Because there is so much we need to talk about and I'm not leaving until we do."

"Then I hope you can afford the room because I have to

check out in the morning and that's not nearly enough time to discuss whatever we have to discuss."

"Fine. Be stubborn." I lower myself to the bed next to her but remain on top of the blankets. I take a few deep breaths before deciding to answer her question and hope she'll feel like talking after she hears what I have to say. "I'm here because I love you. I love you, Til, so goddamn much. Yes, Iz told me where you were." I scrub a hand over my face. "If I'm being honest, I came here with the singular goal of yelling and fighting and demanding that you come home."

"And now?"

"When I got here, I met Marv." She smiles at the mention of him. "He knew me on sight. You've talked about me. You've thought about me." I nod toward the discarded letter at the foot of the bed. "Clearly. But then you came out of that bathroom drunker than shit and all my anger fled because all I wanted to do was take care of you."

"I can take care of myself," she snaps.

"Yeah, yeah you can. But don't you get it? That doesn't matter. I know that you can handle yourself. I know that you're a grown woman and don't need a man, any man, to take care of you. Doesn't change the fact that I want to. I *need* to. Because I love you."

"You didn't need to when you left."

"You told me to go," I snarl, unable to reign in my temper. "You stood right outside that door," I say pointing to the barrier between us and the hallway. "And you told me that you supported me, that you wanted me to go because you didn't want to be the one to hold me back."

"I was lying!" she shouts back. "Jesus, Isaiah, I fucking lied to you. I knew you weren't going to change your mind. And I was not going to be the reason you weren't focused and got yourself killed. I wasn't going to be the person to hold you back."

"Newsflash, Til. I'm fucking alive and I shouldn't be!"

Images of my men lying on the ground, burned, bloody and dead flash before me. I can see Bruno's face as he gives me a hard time about women. I can picture Gordy and Philip and Seth as they laugh at Bruno and me. I can see all of their faces as they rest in their caskets. I can see the faces of their wives, parents, girlfriends, their fucking children, as tears flow.

"Hey, Isaiah." I hear Tillie calling my name but that's crazy because she's back home, safe and away from the war.

Someone touches me on the arm, and I whirl around to see who it is. My vision clears and Tillie comes into focus. We're both standing next to the bed, her naked and me now covered in sweat.

"Where'd you go just now?"

I shake my head to clear it further. "Nowhere. I'm right here."

"Seriously? You expect me to open up and talk but the second I ask you a question that makes you uncomfortable, you shut me out."

She twists away from me and stalks to her bag, lifting it off the floor and throwing it down on the mattress. She yanks the zipper open and digs around until she pulls out a pair of shorts and a tee. She covers herself from me but there's one thing she can't hide, especially in shorts. Her scars.

"I'll let you in if you let me in," I taunt, nodding toward her legs.

"They're nothing." She crawls under the blanket and covers herself even further, as if doing so will erase the marks from my memory.

"Bullshit." I yank the blanket back and grip her knee so she can't pull away from me. "The only thing that does that is a razor. And I can't imagine anyone else did it to you because the scars are too even, too perfect. So, tell me Til, what the fuck did you do?"

Rather than answer, she claws at my hands, pounds my chest, anything and everything she can to push me away, she does. And I let her. Because just like me, she's got pent up rage that she needs to let out. I had Liam to pummel. And Tillie has me.

"You fucking left," she cries as she continues to lash out. "You left and you didn't come back. Not even when I begged you to come back. I wanted to die, believe me, but these aren't about death. They're about a physical pain that somehow lessened the emotional pain. Even if only for a few minutes. I'd have done anything to make it go away. I'd have done anything to get you back. And nothing fucking worked!"

Tillie sobs but stops attacking me and I pull her into my chest and rock her while she cries.

"Aw, Til," I croon. "I'd give anything to go back in time and do things differently."

Her crying slows to a wet hiccup. "That's just it, Isaiah. You could have. I gave you every opportunity to come home, to make things right. I begged you to come home, even if just for a visit."

"What are you talking about?" I ask, genuinely confused. "I never heard from you after that day. I thought you hated me."

"I wrote you every day for the longest time. Eventually, the letters slowed down but at the year mark, I wrote one begging you to meet me here, in this room. Well, guess what? I came. You didn't."

"I never got any letters, Til." She looks at me incredulously. "I swear, I didn't get a single one. I got letters from everyone but you."

"Whatever."

"What did they say?"

"Everything. They said everything."

"Kind of like that one?" I nod at the other letter again. "Were they like that?"

"I guess. Maybe." She sighs. "Not really. I write those every year but never send them. They're for me. A way to vent all my pain that builds up throughout the year."

"What do you do with them?"

"Keep em." She leans forward to dig in her bag again and pulls out a stack of papers. "Here, you can read them if you want. There's one from every year there."

I take the offered letters but don't read them. I will but not now, not when I'd rather hear the words from her own mouth.

"Sum them up for me," I plead. "Please."

"I can't, Isaiah." She presses her hand against her chest. "It hurts too much."

"It hurts because you've kept it all in for so long. Talk to me, Til. I'm here now and I want everything you have to give. The good, the bad, the painful. All of it."

She's silent for several long moments, looking around the room, everywhere but at me. When her eyes finally meet mine, I know that we're going to make it. She can say whatever she wants but her eyes don't lie.

"I fucking love you. Is that what you want to hear?"

"Only if you mean it."

"I do mean it. That's the problem. You read the letter I wrote earlier so don't pretend you don't know what my fears are."

"I'm not pretending. I know what you wrote but there was a lot that you didn't say. For instance, are you willing to try, despite the fear, to have the life we always wanted? Are you willing to risk it?"

"I don't know."

"Yes, you do. I know you, Til. You're the most stubborn woman I've ever met, the most determined. If you want something bad enough, nothing will stop you. So," I pause, wanting to get this right. "Will you risk it? Because I will. Just jump in with both feet with me and I promise you won't regret it."

"What if you leave again?"

"I won't. I know that you don't believe me, but we can spend forever going back and forth with what ifs. The only way to alleviate that fear is to push through and let me prove it to you."

"Shit, Isaiah." She closes her eyes and without opening them, she says, "Okay."

"Yeah?"

"I'm not promising anything." Her lids flutter open. "I can't promise that I'll never worry or that all of my fears are gone. I can't promise that I'll never bring up the past or let it get to me. But I'll try."

"That's all I ask."

23

TILLIE

"What time is check out?"

I curl into Isaiah's side. After I agreed to give us a real shot, we talked until we both fell asleep. I feel his skin against mine, so I know he woke up at some point and stripped down to his boxer briefs. Sunlight streams in through the curtains and the last thing I want to think about is checking out.

"Eleven."

I trace the outline of his six-pack abs, running my fingertips along the line of the fabric. Isaiah twitches slightly and a smile curves my lips.

"How about we stay another day?"

"I'd be okay with that."

"Good. I already called down to the front desk and asked Marv to book us for another night."

"I bet he had a lot to say about that," I tease.

"Not really. The only thing he said was 'It's about time' and then he hung up."

I can't stop the laugh that bubbles out of me. Isaiah joins in and by the time we pull ourselves together, I forget what we're even laughing about. I still have questions for Isaiah but didn't want to push it last night. This morning, I can't hold back.

I sit up, folding my legs beneath me and trace the outline of his tattoo on the underside of his bicep.

"Will you tell me about your last mission?"

Isaiah's eyes darken and he looks away from me. At first, I think he's going to lash out, get angry and refuse to talk, but he surprises me.

"It was a routine mission," he starts. "We'd been on hundreds like it. Seek and destroy basically. Our target was a human trafficker. You can understand why then I got so focused. Actually, I was obsessed. I prepared for that mission for months. I begged for it to be assigned to my team. I got what I wanted." He lets his eyes drift closed. "And my team got dead."

I watch as he wrestles with his emotions. He doesn't move, other than to run a hand through his hair or to fist them in the pillow, no doubt to release some anger.

"It was a bombing. We'd cleared a small village and had relaxed a bit as we made the trek to where our target was supposed to be. Bruno," He looks at me. "He was one of my guys. Anyway, Bruno was giving me a hard time about women and we were having fun. At least, as much fun as you can when on a mission. My men were great about that. We could laugh and joke without taking our eyes off the prize. It helped keep us sane."

"Sounds like a great group of guys."

"They are... were." Isaiah heaves a sigh. "I don't remember the moments leading up to the explosion. Just an intense heat and being thrown. I woke up to a massive fireball and a dead team." He swipes at the wetness on his cheeks. "I have no idea how, but I managed to get them all to the extraction point.

Never leave a man behind. I didn't. I didn't leave a single one."

"I'm so sorry, Isaiah." I wrap my arms around him and hold on.

"I woke up in a hospital and didn't remember how I got there. The nurse had to tell me. I tried to get over it, to move on. For a year, I tried. And then the military booted me. I couldn't perform my job because of the PTSD. I was a mess. So, I came home."

"And then everything happened with your dad and me."

"Til, it's been one shitstorm after another for over a year. The one good thing in it all is you. I thought about you every single day since I left for the military. I know you didn't want to be the person that kept me going, but you were. You always have been. Hell, you always will be."

"I think we're both due for a little happiness."

"You can say that again."

I rise up to my knees and throw a leg over his, straddling him.

"How about I show you instead?"

Isaiah's mouth descends on mine in a flash. His tongue darts out and tangles with mine. Heat pools between my thighs and I grind against his growing cock. Before I can register what he's doing, he lifts me off of him and sheds his boxer briefs in quick succession.

He rolls me to my back and straddles my hips. My pussy clenches, needing to be filled by him. Isaiah leans down and sucks my bottom lip in between his teeth and nips. I roll my hips forward, begging for him to give me what I want but he pulls his hips away.

"Not yet, Til. Not yet."

Isaiah deepens the kiss, taking every moan that escapes into his mouth and using it to fuel the raging inferno between us. I reach between our bodies and wrap my fist around his cock, alternating between squeezing and tugging. Pre-cum beads on the tip and I swirl it around with my thumb.

"I need you, Isaiah," I beg.

"I'm right here."

He moves from my mouth and slides down to line his lips up with my tits. He tweaks a nipple, rolling his between his fingers, and sucks the other one into his wet mouth. The contrast between the two is intense and I buck my hips in response.

He moves his free hand down between us and circles my clit. I'm wet and ready for him and still, he doesn't give me what I want. He shifts away from my breasts and slides further down my body, settling between my thighs. He lifts my legs to drape them over his shoulders.

He blows against my clit for a second before touching it with the tip of his tongue. I cry out and he increases the speed and pressure. He dips a finger into my pussy and crooks it in just the way I like it. Between his finger and his tongue, I'm on the verge of an orgasm of epic proportions.

"Ah, god, please, Isaiah."

I thread my fingers through his hair and pull, trying to get him to go where I want him to go. He doesn't. Instead, he adds a second finger and eats me like a starving man. The pleasure builds and builds until it has nowhere to go.

"Fu-uuck!" I shout.

My hips buck, my knees lock against his head and still, he doesn't slow down. He licks me until I'm a puddle of sated bliss beneath him. When my legs fall open, he removes his fingers and pulls away.

He sits up and, while locking eyes with me, sucks his fingers clean. He crawls up my body and begins kissing me again. I can feel his hand between us, fisting his cock, but I'm so satisfied, it doesn't necessarily register what he's doing.

"You ready?" he asks between kisses.

"Mmm." That's the only thing I'm capable of saying.

The tip of his dick presses against my opening and when he thrusts in, my eyes fly open and I throw my head back.

"Shit, you're bigger than I remember."

Isaiah doesn't move, a startled look on his face. "Am I hurting you?"

"Hell, no." I dig my fingernails into his ass. "I need you. Fuck me, Isaiah."

That's all it takes for him to glide out and thrust back in. He fucks me with so much force that he pushes me up the bed until I hit the headboard. Still, I don't let him stop. I meet him, thrust for thrust, moaning and clawing at him the entire time.

"Holy shit," he breaths. "So damn good."

Isaiah's hips fly and every thrust in is to the hilt. Fire curls in my belly as my orgasm builds. I don't want to soar without him, but I may not be able to stop myself.

"Gonna come," I moan.

The second the words are out of my mouth, Isaiah thrusts one last time and his body stiffens as he pulses inside of me. My pussy clenches and we both shout out our release.

He collapses on top of me and we lay there in a heap of sweaty flesh. My breathing is ragged, and his heart is beating wildly. I remove my hands from his ass and let them fall to my sides. After several minutes, he lifts himself up on his elbows and smiles lazily.

"That was so much better than it was when we were seventeen."

I can't stop the very unladylike snort that escapes. Isaiah's eyes widen and he rolls to his side. I twist my body to throw a leg over his and rest my head on his chest.

"At seventeen, we were clumsy as hell. It was great then but yes, it's un-fucking-believable now."

Isaiah places a kiss on the top of my head and wraps his arm around me. He's quiet for a long time and when I can't take the silence, I rise up on my elbow.

"What are you thinking?" I ask, almost dreading the answer.

He looks at me with such intensity and I have to resist the urge to look away from his scrutiny.

"I didn't come here to fuck, Til." His tone is extremely serious, somber. "You have to know that."

"I didn't think you had." I cup his cheek. "Where's this coming from?"

"You're not the only one who's scared, ya know. I'm terrified of doing or saying the wrong thing, of pushing you away."

"We're a pair, aren't we?"

"You're the only person I want to be a pair with."

He averts his gaze and I gently guide it back to me. "I need you to look at me when I say this, okay?" He nods. "I love you. I always have. I always will. I know things aren't perfect right now and we both still have some shit to process, but we will." I take a deep breath. "I promise to let you in and let you help me with my crap, but you have to promise the same. This can't be one-sided."

"I promise I'll try." His eyes well up and it breaks my heart. "I've got so much shit in my head, Til. Scary shit. But I'll let you in if you can handle it. Just don't leave me. Don't walk away if things get hard or if I'm an asshole sometimes. Promise me. I need you to promise me that you'll never—"

"I promise."

I press my lips to his, making sure that everything in me flows through the kiss. At first, it's sweet, slow, powerful but it shifts quickly to fast and frenzied. I climb on top of Isaiah and sink down on his cock, savoring the way he stretches and fills me.

I lean forward, letting my hair cascade around our faces. While I rock my hips, he slowly thrusts up and pulls out, thrusts up and pulls out. Our foreheads touch and we stare into each other's eyes.

"I love you, Isaiah."

"I love you, too, Til."

We spend the next hour expressing just how much.

24

ISAIAH

The wind whips across my face as I ride down the highway. Tillie's on her Harley, just behind me and while I would rather she be on Nyx with her thighs gripping me and her arms around me, the sight of her on her Harley is incredible. Curly blonde hair flies in the wind and she has a perpetual smile of pure joy.

When I was driving to the hotel, I had no idea how it would turn out. I fully expected having to drag Tillie out, kicking and screaming, but I'm glad it didn't come to that. We talked for hours, once we came up for air, and it felt like old times, like I had my best friend back.

I see a sign for the next exit and glance back to see Tillie nodding her head at me. She knows me so well. We ate breakfast with Marv this morning and I learned a lot about this woman of mine. Mostly that, even when I thought she hated me, she loved me more than life itself and made it known, at least to him.

We pull into a Steak N' Shake and park. Both needing to stretch, we walk around for a few minutes before heading inside to eat. It's the middle of the afternoon so it's not crowded. We place our orders and wait for the food.

"Have you heard from anyone at the club?" she asks.

"What do you think?" I ask, jokingly.

"Let me guess." She puts her finger to her chin like she's thinking hard. "Isabelle text asking if I was okay and Liam text asking when you're coming back. Oh, and both our dads tried to call but didn't leave voicemails."

"You got it."

"So predictable."

"Yeah, but it's kind of nice." I lean back in the booth. "I had no idea what coming home was going to bring but knowing that some things never change is, I don't know, freeing somehow."

"I'm sorry about punching you." She grins.

"No, you're not. But it's okay. I deserved it."

"Here ya go, folks." The waitress sets our plates in front of us. "Can I get you anything else?"

"No, we're good."

"No, thank you."

Tillie and I speak at the same time.

"Okay. Enjoy your food. I'll check back with you in a bit."

We dig into our food. Tillie practically moans with each bite. She always did love their burgers and string fries with cheese. When both of our plates are clean, I pay the bill and we head outside.

"We've only got about two hours left until we're home. Are you good for that stretch or do you want another break at some point?" I know she has to be sore from all of our activities and I don't want her to overdo it.

"I'm good. I'm ready to be—" Her cell phone rings, cutting her off. She glances at the screen and her face reddens. "Jesus, he doesn't quit."

I stick my hand out, silently asking her to hand me the

phone and she does without hesitation. I press the answer button and then put it on speakerphone.

"Hey, Henry," I say. "These phone calls really gotta stop, man."

"Why do you have Tillie's phone?" he asks incredulously.

"I don't think that's really any of your business. What do you want?"

"I need to speak to Tillie. Put her on the phone."

"Not gonna happen. She clearly doesn't want to speak to you, otherwise, she would have answered herself. Just tell me what you want, and I'll be sure to give her the message."

"I text her the other day and she never responded. I just wanted to be sure she was okay."

"She's fine. I've made sure of that." I can't resist the little dig and Tillie rolls her eyes at me.

Henry's breathing intensifies and I can picture his preppy ass bristling on the other end of the line.

"Let her know that Mark got out of the county jail today. The case was assigned to me and I did my best to have bail denied but he's got too many connections. She needs to be careful."

Every muscle in my body tightens and I grip the phone tighter. Tillie straightens at the news and shifts so she's closer to me. I pull her against me as if somehow that will make it all better.

"I'll let her know."

"Be sure that you do. I'd hate for anything to happen to her. She's been... *distracted* lately. She can't be too careful with this guy."

"Henry, that sounds like a bit of a threat. You better not be threatening her."

"It's not a threat," he snaps. "It's a warning. Mark is dangerous."

"Thanks for the info. I'll pass it on."

Without waiting for a response, I end the call. I pull out my own cell phone and call Liam.

"Please tell me you're on your way home," he says by way of a greeting.

"We are. What's up?"

"Henry has been calling and stopping by. Dude, I don't know what the fuck his issue is but if I have to see his ugly mug one more time, I'm gonna snap him in half." The anger in Liam's voice matches my own. "Fucker pretends to give a shit about Tillie but he's just nosy."

"I hear ya," I reply. "That's why I called. He's nosy as hell but it turns out he actually had some info."

"Jesus," he breathes. "Lay it on me."

"Mark, that guy from the other day at the shelter, got out of jail. I need you to go to the shelter and stick close. I don't trust the guy further than I can throw him. And he's a fat fuck so I couldn't throw him far."

"I can do that. I'll leave right now."

There's noise in the background and I know Liam's serious about leaving right this minute.

"Take Noah and Adam with you. It's a big building and the more protection, the better."

"Got it." I hear his bike fire up. "Let me know when you get home. I'll check in every few hours with updates."

"Thanks, man."

"Hey, don't thank me. It's what we do."

"Right. It is."

I disconnect the call and turn to face Tillie. She's straddling her bike, scrolling through her phone. I close the distance between us and look over her shoulder. She's texting back and forth with Karen and from the look of it, they've got their ducks in a row.

"Let her know that Liam, Noah, and Adam are on their way."

She types out a quick text saying just that and then follows it with one telling her that she'll check in when we get home. When she's done, she puts her phone in her saddlebags and revs her engine.

"Let's get home."

I give her a quick peck.

"It's going to be okay. I promise."

I don't normally promise things I'm not sure I can follow through with but if there's anything I know for certain it's that I love Tillie and I will do whatever it takes to make sure that everything is okay.

25

TILLIE

"Is it ever going to end?"

Isaiah looks up from his laptop. He's in the library in the main house and I tried to wait for him to get home but couldn't. We've been home for a few days, and nothing has happened with Mark. Isaiah has kept the added protection at the shelter and security has been stepped up at the club but I'm still on edge.

"What?" he asks.

"The danger." I straddle his lap and rest my arms on his shoulders. "I'm over it. Always looking over my shoulder. Not being able to go anywhere or do anything without a damn shadow."

"I'm your shadow," he teases.

"And you're the best shadow but I need my life back." At his confused look, I clarify. "I don't mean that I want you to leave. I just want to be able to go to work or the shelter or hell, the damn grocery store. I've always done what I wanted when I wanted, and I can't do that."

"I know it's hard, but it won't last forever." Isaiah's hands work their way under my shirt, and he slides them up my back. "If Henry can't get the job done then I'll make sure that Mark is taken care of."

I tilt my head, trying to determine if he's serious or not. Judging by the scowl on his face and the way his fingers are digging into my flesh, I'd say he's dead serious. Quite literally, too.

Needing to change the subject and suspecting that Isaiah needs that too, I wiggle my ass against him.

"You about done here?" I bob my eyebrows up and down.

"I am now."

He leans around me and slams his laptop shut and then lifts me up as he stands. I lock my ankles at the small of his back as he carries me toward the door. I expect him to keep walking but instead, he kicks the door shut and flips the lock.

"Here?" I ask.

"Can't wait."

He fits his lips to mine and strides back to the desk where he sets me on the edge and wedges himself between my legs. Gripping the hem of my shirt, he tears it off over my head and buries his face between my breasts. I reach down and unbutton his jeans, working them over his hips until they pool at his feet.

"Now you."

He lifts me up enough that I can shimmy my jeans and panties over my hips. When they're at my thighs, he drops me back down onto the desk and yanks them down my legs, whisking them and my boots off at the same time.

He wastes no time as he lines himself up and slams into me. There are other club members in the house, so I know it's going to be a quick fuck. I hang on to him so I don't scoot across the wood.

Isaiah licks his finger and presses it against my clit for

added stimulation and the combination of that and his cock send rockets ricocheting through me. My walls clench and spasm around him. He doesn't slow his pace until he throbs inside of me and crashes over the edge.

"Goddamn, woman."

He grabs a tissue and cleans us both up before pulling up his jeans and handing me mine. I hop off the desk and get dressed.

"I think we both needed that little distraction." I wink at him and he laughs.

"Little?"

I glance down at his junk and am surprised to see a bulge pressing against his zipper already. "Okay, it's far from little."

"Damn straight."

"Can we go home now?"

"I wish I could. I've got a few things to wrap up. Why don't you see if Isabelle wants to come keep you company?"

"I already tried that. She was getting ready for a date. Hence why I'm here."

"She's got a date? Who? Where are they going? How come I didn't know about this?"

"Probably because you'd have hit her with all of the same questions." I dodge out of the way when he tries to grab me and pick me up. He chases me around the library but I'm faster than him and he doesn't catch me. When we both stop, I answer what I can. "Yes, Iz has a date. His name is Josh and she met him at Dusty's. She said they're going to see a movie, but I didn't ask what one."

"I don't know anyone named Josh." He narrows his eyes and his consternation is not only funny but endearing.

"I mean, somehow she managed to stay safe and alive for eight years when you weren't vetting her dates." I grab his hand and thread my fingers through his. "C'mon, Isaiah.

She's smart and she's allowed to go out and have fun. She'll be fine."

"You're right," he conceded. "I'm sorry. Everything that's happened with your attack and Mark has me on edge." His eyes widen. "Please tell me you at least told her not to call an Uber."

"She promised me she wouldn't. She said if it came down to it, she'd call me. But I'm pretty sure that she's meeting Josh at the theater so she has her own transportation."

"Smart."

"Exactly."

"Okay, smartass." He grabs my ass cheeks and squeezes. "Head on home and I'll finish up here. If you stay, you'll distract me."

"Fine." I drag out the word dramatically just to give him a hard time. "I'll see you at home."

With that, I leave so he can do what he needs to do. Rather than go to my place, I head to my parent's house. I haven't gotten to spend much time with them lately and I miss Lila. When I arrive, my sister comes running out of the house.

"Where have you been?" she demands, stopping short of jumping on my bike. "You never come over anymore."

"You can come to my place, ya know," I remind her. We used to hang out a lot but with her in college, it's harder to find the time.

"I know but Isaiah is there." She winks at me. "I'm afraid I'll walk in on something. Once was enough." She says, referring to a time she caught us in one of the fields on the property back in high school and mock shudders.

"Oh, shut the fuck up." I swat at her, but she dodges my hand. "How's school going?" I sling my arm around her shoulder, and we head inside. "Still getting good grades?"

"Duh." She throws her head back and laughs and it feels like we haven't skipped a beat since the last time we hung out.

"So, little sister, is there a flavor of the month?"

"Hell, no. Men suck." Lila's demeanor changes so fast I have a hard time keeping up. "Jack's a dick and I hope he rots."

"What did he do? Isaiah and I can make him suffer if we have to."

"That's how it is, huh?"

"What?"

"You and Isaiah are a thing now? Like, for real or just playing house or something?"

We walk arm and arm through the front door and our parents are sitting on the couch, talking about something. Both stop talking when they hear us, and my dad gives me a pointed look.

"That's a good question, Lila," he says before fixing his gaze on me. "How are things with Isaiah, Peanut?"

I shrug as if it's no big deal. "They're good."

"That's it?" Mom asks. "Just 'good'? He did join you at that hotel and you were gone a day longer than normal."

"That is true."

"Peanut, are you happy?"

I think about the question and for the first time in a very long time, I can answer honestly. "Very happy, Daddy."

"Then that's all that matters."

That's what I love about my dad. He can worry about me and he'll definitely give me his opinion if he feels so inclined, but at the end of the day, if I'm happy then he's happy for me.

"Why don't you all come to dinner some night soon? I know Isaiah would really like to catch up with all of you and we didn't really get to do that on Sunday."

"That would be great," Mom beams. "I've got a few things to do in town tomorrow but what about the day after?"

"Sounds good. I'll double-check with Isaiah when he gets home later."

Mom and Dad exchange a knowing glance, but I choose to ignore it. Let them have their fun. Lila, on the other hand, isn't so quiet about her opinions.

"I'll come to dinner, but I don't feel like watching you two suck face, so make sure he knows that."

"Jesus, Lila," I mumble. "Grow up."

She sticks her tongue out at me and I know she knows I'm only kidding. It's my prerogative as the older sister. And she'll tell you it's hers as the younger sister to relentlessly tease me and give me a hard time about everything.

"Anyway, I gotta run. I've got some work to catch up on and I'd like to get as much of it done before Isaiah gets home." I glare at Lila when she opens her mouth. "Not a word."

"You're no fun," she pouts.

"I know." I give my mom and dad a hug and head out the door. "Love you guys."

I hear their 'love you too's' as I job down the steps and hop on my bike. The drive to my place is fairly quick and when I get home, I waste no time getting to work. I've got a few phone calls to return and files to prep for court and I don't feel like being stuck at it all night.

I get lost in depositions and discovery packets and before I know it, two hours have passed. I glance at my phone to see if Isaiah texted and I missed it but there's nothing there, so I text him.

Me: Home soon?

Isaiah: Leaving now

I smile to myself and race upstairs to jump in the shower, ignoring whatever work I was doing. I'm hoping Isaiah will join me when he gets home. Within a few minutes, the Harley's engine roars, and I shiver in anticipation.

"Tillie?" Isaiah calls out to me when he comes inside.

"Up here," I shout.

His boots thud on the stairs and the bathroom door crashes open. The shower curtain is yanked open and even though I'm expecting it, I shriek. He rips his clothes off and steps under the spray with me.

His lips capture mine and he lifts me up to spin me around and pin me against the wall. He's inside of me so fast I barely have time to blink. His weight, combined with my legs grip around him, holds me in place and he brings my arms above my head and holds them to the tile. The friction between our bodies brings us to climax quickly and when we're done, I slide down him, but my legs are so wobbly that he has to hold me to keep me upright.

"Hi," I purr.

"Hey."

"I'm glad you're home."

"Me too. But now that we've had dessert, I'm starving." He chuckles at his own joke. "What's for dinner?"

"I figured we could ride into town and grab something."

"Sounds good to me."

We finish in the shower and get dressed. It takes me a few minutes longer than him to get ready but not much. When I get downstairs, he's standing by the door, tapping his foot like he's been waiting hours.

"It's about time. I thought I was gonna starve waiting on you."

"Shut up, asshole. You've been down here for ten minutes."

"True." He eyes me up and down. "It was worth the wait."

I glance down at my jeans and long-sleeved tee. It's simple but it'll keep me warm on the ride. Hey, if he likes it, who am I to argue.

The ride into town is nice, just the two of us like old times. Isaiah is tense but I chalk it up to him constantly being on alert for danger. With Mark out of jail, going into town might not be the best idea but he's not stupid enough to try anything in public.

Dinner is quick, just burgers from the local joint, but they're delicious and very filling. By the time we get back home, I'm beat, but I've got a little bit more work to do. Isaiah relaxes on the sofa and puts an action movie on.

Several more hours pass before I can stop for the night. I shut my computer down and go to join him on the couch. He's stretched out with his legs dangling over the end and sound asleep. I pull the blanket off the back and cover him with it. I don't have the heart to wake him up. He's had a long day between club business and me and deserves to get some rest.

I curl up in the overstuffed chair, not wanting to go upstairs and be away from him. Maybe it's silly but now that we're back together, I'm almost afraid to let him out of my sight for too long.

I start to doze off but am jolted awake by my cell phone beeping on the coffee table. I quickly lean over to grab it so it doesn't wake Isaiah up and see notifications for several texts. The number reads unknown and that alone makes the hairs on the back of my neck stand up.

Unknown: U look good on the back of a bike

Unknown: U can straddle me anytime

I scroll through a litany of lewd texts, each one more suggestive than the one before it.

When I reach the very last text, an involuntary shudder rolls through me.

Unknown: Ur week is up. I'm going hunting

26

ISAIAH

"This sick fuck needs dealt with."

Aiden's pacing back and forth in Tillie's living room. It's the middle of the night and her house is filled to the brim with club members, who all raced here when I sent out the mass text.

"I agree." I rest my hand on Aiden's shoulder and squeeze. "He's not going to get away with this. I don't give a shit who his family is."

"He's gotten away with this kind of thing for years," Tillie reminds me. "What makes you think you're going to make a difference?"

"He'll do what needs doing, regardless of the law." I glance at Pops and nod. "My son will not let Mark get to you or anyone else."

"Look," Tillie starts. "I want Mark out of the picture as much as all of you but what about his kids? What will that do to them?"

"Til, what'll *Mark* do to them if he's not dealt with?" I go to her and pull her in for a hug. She's got such a big heart and doesn't want anyone to be hurt. Unfortunately, that's not always possible or what's best. "It's not just you he's threatened. It's you, your staff, his wife and kids... pretty much anyone he can threaten, he's threatened. I wish it wouldn't have come to this too, but it has."

She fists her hands in my shirt and nods against my chest. "Doesn't mean I have to like it."

"You're right, Peanut," Aiden says as he steps up to her and grips her shoulder. "None of us like this situation and not just because one of our own is in trouble. It's a nasty part of life and it's what we all signed on for."

"Maybe I could talk to—"

"That's not gonna happen," I growl.

"Then what's the plan?" she cries. "Because I need to warn Susie so she can prepare the kids for the fallout."

"For starters, you're gonna work from home until he's no longer a threat."

"The hell I am!" she shouts back at me. "The shelter is safer than this place is, and you know it. You all do." She turns in a circle to include everyone in her argument. "I made sure that it was because those families have been through enough." She returns her attention to only me and glares. "Isaiah, I'll do almost anything you ask me but not this. I will not abandon them and hide away like a pussy."

I glance at Aiden and then my dad and Griffin, silently asking for their input. All three of them nod and I have to bite my tongue not to lash out at them.

"Fine. But no overtime or anything like that. You go to work like you normally do and you will always have one of us with you. *Always*, Til. That's not negotiable."

She nods so fast it reminds me of a bobblehead. "Okay. I promise. I'll never be alone." She jumps into my arms, forcing me to catch her. "Thank you."

"Don't thank me," I growl in her ear and then I dip my voice to a whisper. "At least not in front of your dad."

"We all heard that dude," Liam says from five feet away.

I flip him off after setting Tillie on her feet. He returns the gesture, laughing as he does it.

"Tillie, are you sure about this?" Isabelle steps around me and gives her a worried look. "I mean, this guy is dangerous. You've been through so much and I don't want to see anything else happen."

"Iz, you've known me your whole life. When have you ever seen me back down from a fight or hide away from danger?"

"Never, but this is—"

"I'll be fine, Iz." Tillie envelops my sister in a hug. "Your brother will make sure of it."

Isabelle nods and then whirls around to face me. "If anything happens to her, you'll wish I'd been one of those twins that killed the other in the womb."

The scary part of her threat is that she's right. She'll make me suffer. Along with everyone else in the room. This is one mission I can't fuck up.

Images of burned bodies flash in my mind but I shake them away. Nothing is going to happen. This isn't the middle of fucking nowhere and I've got the best people I know backing me up. My Seal team was incredible, but they weren't my club.

"Okay, let's get comfortable everyone," I say with authority. "It's going to be a long night."

The next few hours are spent working out a schedule for protection detail for a month. I'm hoping we won't need it that long, but I'd rather be prepared.

Noah is taking the first shift when Tillie goes to the shelter tomorrow. I let Tillie convince me to meet with a therapist to address my PTSD and my first appointment is tomorrow. There's no way she'll let me reschedule, not for her. I don't like it, but I have to put my faith in my club.

Once a plan is in place, every minute of every day is accounted for, no one makes a move to go home. I don't know if it's the adrenaline from preparing for battle or if we all just have so much to catch up on, but it doesn't matter. There is nowhere I'd rather be than right here with my woman and my family.

At five in the morning, people start to trickle out and make their way home. Some will grab a few hours of sleep, others will simply chug some coffee and mentally prepare for the day. When the last person leaves, I carry Tillie upstairs and love her into oblivion.

"I'm gonna just go ahead and suck your dick."

My eyes pop open at the sultrily whispered promise. I lift my head and see the top of Tillie's blonde hair as she glides down my torso, leaving a trail of wet heat in her wake.

When her lips graze the tip of my throbbing cock, it jumps as if to say 'hello, here I am'. She sucks it into her mouth and works her mouth up and down, deep-throating me like a champ. I don't know what's hotter: her actions or watching her as she sucks me off.

Tillie swirls her tongue around the head, and I have my answer. Definitely her actions. My head falls back against the pillows and I fist my hands in her hair, unable to stop myself. She moans and the vibrations travel down my cock and I shiver uncontrollably.

"Your mouth is heaven," I say on a moan.

Tillie increases her speed and tightens her lips around me. Her hand cups my balls and that sends me over the edge. I try to pull out but she holds me still, swallowing down my cum without missing a beat.

I pull her up my body and meld my mouth with hers. Her

fingernails dig into my flesh for a second before she pushes herself back and ends the kiss.

"I know it's not what you wanna hear but I have to go to work."

"You're right. I don't want to hear it." I try to urge her back toward my face but she resists. I heave a sigh. "Fine. But I'll pay you back for that later."

"I'm gonna hold you to that."

She winks and climbs off the bed, sashaying naked out of the bedroom.

"Damnit, Tillie, if you keep it up, I'm going to tie you to the bed and have my way with you."

"Later," she calls over her shoulder.

The bathroom door closes behind her and the pipes groan when she turns on the shower. I shake my head at my little minx. She drives me insane but for the most part, it's in the best possible ways.

I roll to my side and snag my cell off the nightstand. A text from Noah indicates that he's on his way and I'm suddenly grateful that Tillie resisted me. No need for us to get caught.

I respond to his text with a thumbs-up emoji and as soon as I hit send, another text comes through. It's from an unknown number and my insides twist into a knot.

It's Henry. Tried to text Tillie but her phone must be off. I just want to make sure that someone is going to be at the shelter with her. There's talk of more threats by Mark and I'm concerned. I know you hate me but please let me know so I can arrange for someone to be with her if you don't already have that planned.

I want to tell Henry to fuck off, but I take a few deep breaths and reign in the urge. He seems genuinely concerned about Tillie's safety and the least I can do for the poor sap is let him know she's safe. Hopefully, that'll be enough to keep him away.

Got it handled. One of my guys will be with her all day.

I hit send and put the whole exchange out of my mind as I get up and throw some shorts and a t-shirt on. I'll shower after Noah picks Tillie up. The shower shuts off and a minute later, Tillie struts through the bedroom door butt naked.

"Noah's going to be here any minute," I warn her. "I'd rather he not see you like that." I eye her up and down. "It's all mine."

Tillie races to throw some clothes on, a pair of jeans and a sweater, her typical attire for when she works at the shelter. I asked her about it once and she told me that she never wanted the residents to feel like she looked down on them so unless it was a court day, she didn't wear dress clothes.

The knock on the door pulls me from my musings and I go downstairs to let Noah in.

"Morning."

I shake Noah's offered hand. "Morning. Thanks for sticking with her today."

"Don't mention it. Tillie's always been great with me, even when she probably shouldn't have been. I'd do anything for her."

Before I can question him about that ominous statement, Tillie breezes down the stairs and greets him with a kiss on the cheek and a hug. Jealousy hits me hard. They clearly have a connection that I somehow hadn't noticed until just now and I hate the thought of someone else sharing that bond with her. It seems like Noah holds on a little longer than necessary and jealousy morphs into anger.

"Okay, that's enough," I bark.

Tillie pulls away and laughs at me. "If I'm not mistaken, I'd say you're jealous."

"Of course, I'm jealous. I thought I'd made it clear that you're mine." I glare at Noah. "Someone doesn't seem to have gotten the memo."

"No need to worry, Prez. I love Tillie, but not like that. She's uh, well…" Noah rubs the side of his nose, very clearly uncomfortable.

"She's not his type," Tillie finishes for him. "I don't have the right equipment."

"Oh." I breathe a sigh of relief.

"Is that going to be a problem?" Noah asks quietly.

"Fuck no," I assure him. "Why the hell would it be?"

Noah shrugs. "Not everyone is open-minded."

"Yeah, well, they should be." I clap him on the back. "You're my brother, both as a veteran and a club member. Who you love isn't going to change that, as long as this club is on that list."

Noah smiles and the tension in the room disappears. I may not know Noah very well yet, but he's family. Simple as that.

"We better get going," Tillie says as she grabs her stuff off of the small table near her front door. "I want to talk to Susie today and I'm hoping to do it while the kids are in school."

"Lead the way."

Noah steps aside to let her precede him out the door.

"Noah," I call when he turns to follow. He glances back at me. "Take care of my girl."

"I will. I promise."

27

TILLIE

"Do you think I should pull the kids out of school?"

The worried look on Susie's face is heartbreaking. She's used to Mark's rage but that doesn't make it easier. And now she's also blaming herself for the danger to everyone else. I've tried to reassure her but to no avail.

"No, I don't think that's necessary. The office has the paperwork stating that you are the only person permitted to pick them up. The school is very good about stuff like that, very cooperative. No need to disrupt the kids any more right now."

She nods but she doesn't look convinced. "Okay. If you really think it'll be okay. What about you? Should you even be here? What if he shows up?"

"If he shows up, ma'am, he's going to get one hell of a surprise," Noah says from his spot at the door. "He won't get through me. Don't worry."

"See, we've thought of everything." Even as I say the words, I can't help but wonder. I trust that Noah will do everything in his power to keep me safe but sometimes there's no protection against a lunatic. "Why don't you go relax before the kids get home? Curt is down for a nap but I'll listen for him in case he wakes up. I know you're exhausted and now that we're here, you don't have to be so vigilant."

"Um, okay." Susie stands from the chair but makes no move to leave.

"Susie? What is it?" I ask as I stand too.

She throws her arms around me. "Thank you," she says around a sob. "Thank you for everything you've done for me and my kids."

Tears burn the back of my eyes. "You're welcome."

I recognize the need to thank me but I hate that they feel it. I don't do what I do for thanks. I do what I do because I've been where they're at. Or my mom has anyway. If not for her courage and her accepting help, I wouldn't have even been born, let alone lived the life I've lived.

When she finally leaves, Noah stares at me curiously.

"What?" I ask when I can't take his scrutiny.

"You're really good with them."

"I'm really real with them. There's a difference." There's a bite to my tone and I instantly feel bad for that. "Sorry. I just…" I shrug. "I get them, that's all."

"Regardless of the reason, I just thought you should know. I admire you, Tillie."

"Thank you."

"You're welcome." Noah pats his stomach. "Now, can we grab some lunch because I signed up to protect you, not to starve."

The teasing in his tone does the trick and I throw my head back and laugh.

"Yeah, we can eat. I think there are leftovers in the kitchen."

"Sounds go—"

"Oh, let him go get a proper meal."

I whip my head in the direction of the hall and see Henry standing there, smiling.

"What the hell are you doing here? I told you, I don't want to see you outside of your office."

"Relax, Tillie," he cajoles. "I'm just here to deliver some information. I tried to call but you didn't answer."

"I've been busy," I snap.

"Dude, I don't think she wants you here," Noah says, stepping between me and Henry.

"Noah, really? I'm not a stranger." Henry glances between us both. "Tillie, please, can I just have a few minutes of your time?"

"Fine," I snap. "Noah, it's okay. Go to the kitchen and see what you can find to eat. Whatever you want, help yourself."

"Are you sure?" he asks.

"Of course. It's Henry." I glare at my ex. "I don't like him and I sure as hell don't want to see him but we're going to have to talk sooner or later about my case so it might as well be now."

"If you're sure." Noah turns to leave but stops. "If you need anything, Tillie, just holler. I'll hear you." He speaks to me but keeps his glare focused on Henry, the warning clear.

"Got it." I nod at him. "Go, seriously. I'm fine."

When Noah disappears around the corner, Henry huffs out a breath. "What's his problem?"

"You, Henry. You're his problem. In fact, you're mine too. What do you want?"

"How have you been, Tillie?"

"I've been great. Isaiah is taking great care of me."

I cross my arms over my chest. I know I'm being bitchy, but I really don't give a damn. Not only did he insult my way of life and my family, he's made a pest of himself ever since.

"That's good."

His words shock me. It's not the response I was expecting at all. We both stand there, staring at one another for what feels like forever. I'm the first to break the silence when I clear my throat.

"You said you had news. I assume it's about my case."

"Actually, it's about Mark." I narrow my eyes at him. "I told you I was assigned his case. I'm kept up to date on everything going on and wanted to be sure to keep you in the loop, seeing as his family is under your shelter's roof."

"I appreciate that." Even I can concede when someone is just trying to do the right thing. He's annoying but this is business. "So, what's the information?" I prod when he doesn't speak.

"I know that he's sent you threatening texts." Confusion settles in at that bit of information. How the hell does he know that? "We're monitoring his phone," he says, and I realize I voiced my question out loud. "Anyway, his phone has been confiscated so you shouldn't receive any more."

"That's great," I mumble, still trying to digest the fact that he knew about the texts. As far as I know, the prosecutor's office doesn't monitor texts, only calls. "When did that start? The text monitoring?"

Henry looks flustered for a split second and that's all it takes for me to realize there is so much more to this impromptu visit than to provide information.

"Henry, why are you really here?" I take a few steps back, instinctively putting more distance between us. "Answer me!"

"To give you information, like I said." His eye twitches and that's not something I've ever noticed with him before. "What's wrong?" he asks as he takes a step forward.

"You're lying to me. Why?"

I keep walking backward as he continues to advance. I don't dare turn my back on him. I never would have thought that Henry could be violent but now I'm second-guessing everything I thought I knew. There's just something about the way he's acting that isn't right.

"Tillie, baby, I'm not lying."

"Baby? We were together a year and you never once called me 'baby'."

I see the instant the switch flips in him. His face contorts with rage and he balls his hands into fists. He's advancing faster and I turn and break out into a run.

"Noah!" I scream.

Pain radiates through my scalp and I'm dragged backward by my hair. I put my hands up and try to break his grip, but I can't. He's a lot stronger than I thought.

"Tillie, Tillie, Tillie," Henry sing songs. "Why do you have to go and stick your nose where it doesn't belong. If you'd have just turned away Susie and the kids when I advised you to do that, this wouldn't be happening."

"What are you talking about?"

Henry allows me to stand up, but he pulls a butterfly knife from his pocket and expertly flips it open and holds it to my throat to coax me to do as I'm told.

"When they were first referred here, you told me about it in bed that night. I told you not to admit them, that Mark was trouble, but you didn't listen. No, you've gotta be all righteous and help everyone."

I rack my brain for any memory of what he's talking about and it hits me. It was post-sex and we were talking about our days. He said he knew the family well from all of the arrests and court appearances Mark had for assault and domestic violence. I didn't think anything of it at the time because he's the prosecutor. It made sense. But he's right, I didn't listen.

He shoves me while we walk, guiding me toward the

kitchen. Noah never showed so I know that he's gotta be down. The question is how.

"Why do you care so much about this family, about Mark?"

"Because he's my step-brother."

Mark appears in front of me, having stepped through the doorway to the kitchen. I'm looking down the barrel of a sawed-off shotgun and I have no doubt he'll use it.

"You realize we have to kill her now that you told her that," Henry states matter-of-factly, like killing me is the same thing as a Sunday drive. "If she lives, I'll lose my job. If I lose my job, who the fuck is going to keep rescuing your ass?"

My head spins as I try to process everything. I review in my head all of the security protocols we have in place and wonder what failed. Something had to have failed for Mark to get in here unnoticed.

"Where's Noah?" I ask.

"He'll be fine," Mark assures me, but I don't find it reassuring at all. "I think." He looks to Henry. "Bring her in here where we can keep an eye on both of them."

Henry doesn't move so Mark reaches out and yanks me forward. I stumble with the force of his pull but manage to stay on my feet. When we clear the doorway, I see Noah sprawled on his stomach, blood pooling beneath his head.

"What the fuck did you do?" I demand.

I race forward and am thankful that Mark lets me. Dropping to my knees next to Noah, I run my hands over his head looking for his wound. I find the large cut that's oozing blood and am thankful that it's only a cut. Judging by the size, he took a blow to the back of his head with the shotgun. I wish I didn't know that but in my line of work and with the work we do at the club, I've seen more than my fair share of head wounds. Noah will live but he'll have a hell of a headache.

"Where are Susie and the kids?"

Mark yanks me up by my hair and shoves me against the counter. The edge cuts into my back and I bite my lip to keep myself from crying out.

"It's the middle of the day," I say. "Where do you think they are?"

"How the hell should I know? You've got them so twisted up that they're probably not doing anything I'd think they should be doing."

I glance at Henry, who's standing in the doorway like he doesn't have a care in the world.

"Let me ask you something, Henry." I tilt my head. "Was this plan hatched before or after you saw me in the bar that night?"

"Does it matter?" he counters.

"Well, I'd like to know if I was fucking a monster for a full year or only for a few weeks."

Shut up, Tillie.

Henry's cavalier attitude slips and he stalks toward me and slaps me across the face. My mouth fills with a metallic taste and blood trickles from my split lip.

"I'm not a monster," he snarls. He leans in so close our noses are almost touching. "I'm a good brother. You of all people should understand that."

I don't let him get to me and force myself not to back my head up. "I do understand that. What I don't get is how you can let this sick fuck beat on his family and think it's okay."

"It's the only way if a bitch doesn't know her place. I'd have done the same to you eventually. It's in a man's nature to control."

"No, Henry, it's not. If you love someone, you do anything to protect them, to let them know you love them."

"Is that what Isaiah told you? I promise you, Tillie, he'll show his true colors eventually. We all do."

"Both of you, shut the fuck up!" Mark shouts, clearly fed up with the conversation deviating from his plan.

Mark whips me around and grabs me by the back of the head, pushing it forward to slam off of the counter. My head spins with the blow and my vision blurs. He pulls back and gets in my face.

"Where are they?" When I remain silent, he yanks me back just to slam my head again. "I'm going to ask you one more time. Where. Is. Susie?"

"Fuck. You."

I spit and blood splatters on his face. I don't regret saying it, even as he pulls my head back a third time and cracks my face against the stainless steel of the counter. I don't regret it as he let's go and I feel myself falling to the floor.

And I don't regret it as I crumble and lose consciousness.

28

ISAIAH

"How did your appointment go?"

My dad's question is tentative, and I hate that he feels like he needs to tiptoe around the subject of my PTSD. Hell, he has it.

"It was good. I've got another one next week."

"Really? That's good, son."

"Thanks, Pops." I straddle Nyx as I wait at the curb to finish the conversation. "Hey, I tried to call Tillie but got no answer. Same with Noah. Have you heard from them?"

"No." He sighs. "You know how busy she is. She's probably still trying to calm Susie down and Noah's not answering out of respect, I'm sure. Don't worry too much."

"Yeah, you're probably right but...I don't know. Something just doesn't feel right."

"My only advice then is to listen to your gut. You made a great Seal for a reason. You've got good instincts. Head on over to the shelter and check on her. It'll ease your mind."

"That's where I'm headed as soon as we hang up."

The call is disconnected and even as tense as I am, I chuckle. Leave it to Pops to push me.

I fire Nyx up and pull away, pointing her in the direction of the shelter. As I drive, my mind races with all of the possibilities as to why Tillie and Noah aren't answering their phones. When I turn onto the dirt road, I feel my cell vibrate. I don't bother stopping to read it. I'm so close and can read it in a minute.

When I reach the shelter, my heart skips a beat. Henry's Mercedes is parked out front. What the hell is he doing here? I pull my phone from the inside pocket of my cut and my stomach bottoms out. The text is from Karen and the only word she sent is 'blowjob'.

I bend down and grab my Glock out of my boot and also grab a second one out of my saddlebags. The weight of the gun in my hand helps to ground me when I otherwise feel like I'm spiraling out of control.

I dial Liam and put the phone to my ear while I double-check the weapons for full cartridges.

"What's up?"

"Trouble at the shelter. I need you here ASAP."

"Got it."

Liam disconnects the call. Even if he breaks every speed limit, he's twenty minutes out. I can't wait that long, so I make my way around the building to the secret entrance Tillie took me through the last time there was trouble.

I don't know the code, so I take a chance and smash the butt of my gun into the panel. It does the trick and shorts it out, allowing the lock to disengage. I slowly open the door and peek around it. When I verify that the coast is clear, I enter, careful to not make a sound.

As I walk down the hall, I clear each room I pass. I don't bother stopping in Tillie's office because I don't want to waste the time. When I reach the last door on the left, I see the top of Karen's head as she's crouching behind it. I step inside and she jumps up when she spots me.

"Oh, thank god." She breathes what I imagine is a sigh of relief. "I wasn't sure if she told you the danger word or not."

"She did." I glance over my shoulder to make sure we're still alone. "What's going on? I saw Henry's car."

"He's here and so is Mark. From what I heard, they're step-brothers."

"What the hell?"

"I don't know. They've got Tillie and Noah in the kitchen. I heard Tillie scream for Noah so I immediately sent out the alert for residents to go to the panic room. They're all safe."

"Why didn't you go?"

"Because I wanted to be able to let help in when it arrived. I wasn't sure if you had the code to the back door or not. I figured if you didn't, you'd text or call."

"Okay," I nod, processing what she's telling me and simultaneously trying to come up with a plan of attack. "Did you alert the police?"

"Right after I texted you." She shrugs. "I trust you more than them. Anyway, obviously, they aren't here yet."

"What the hell are we paying taxes for if… ya know what? Never mind." I turn to go out the door. "I need you to get to the panic room. Now. I've got this."

"I can't—"

"Karen, it's not up for discussion. I can't worry about you too right now. I need to focus on Tillie and Noah." The indecision on her face prompts my next words. "It's what Tillie would want."

She nods and I leave her, trusting that she'll do as she's told. I continue to clear any room I pass and when I exit that hallway and enter the great room, I can hear voices. Henry and Mark. Henry sounds frazzled but Mark just sounds enraged.

"What the hell did you do that for?" Henry asks.

"You already said we're gonna have to kill her. What's a few more bruises in the process?"

A red haze hovers in my vision. I will kill both of those motherfuckers for hurting her.

"But you're gonna let him live?" Henry again.

Good. Noah's still alive.

"Of course not. But I need one of them alive to get me to Susie and the kids."

I flatten myself against the wall when I'm within five feet of the kitchen door. I have to time this right if I'm going to have any element of surprise. I quiet my mind and force my breathing to even out. I listen closely to their footsteps as they pace. After a few minutes, I'm certain I can tell when they're walking away from the door and when they are close.

After another minute, I hear the thud of their steps recede and I know it's now or never. I walk sideways to the door and lean around to verify that their backs are turned. The second I observe confirmation, I whirl around the corner and squeeze the trigger.

Mark collapses to the floor and Henry whips around to face me.

"What's it gonna be Henry?" I ask. "Are you going to end up dead like your brother?" At his shocked expression, I elaborate. "That's right. I know all about you both." The lie comes easily. I do know about them, but not a lot. Only what I've learned in the last ten minutes. "Dead? Or alive? I know what my choice would be."

Henry looks down at Mark and back up at me. He's scared but he's going to pretend that he's not. What he doesn't understand is I have all the training I need to recognize exactly what he's doing. I may not have seen it before but it's crystal fucking clear now. He's pure evil and I won't hesitate to put him down like a dog if he makes one wrong move.

"I need an answer Henry," I taunt him. "This gun is getting pretty heavy and I'd hate for it to slip or something and accidentally go off."

He swallows audibly as he lifts his hand with the knife in it. I have to will myself not to laugh at him. He still thinks he has a chance of walking out of here. The second that hand moved a fraction of an inch, he sealed his fate.

Henry lunges forward and I pull the trigger, not feeling an ounce of guilt of taking his life. I rush forward and check for a pulse, just to be sure. Both he and Mark are stone-cold dead. Satisfaction slithers through me at the knowledge that I rid the world of their filth.

I crawl to Tillie and put my cheek to her nose to check for breath while simultaneously checking for a pulse.

"Thank fucking Christ," I whisper when I feel both. I glance back to Noah and see his

chest rising and falling so I know he's okay. Returning my attention to Tillie, I lift her into my lap and try to cajole her awake. "C'mon, Til, wake up for me. I need you to wake up."

I've always known I have a calming effect on her but when her eyes flutter open at my command, I realize just how bonded we are.

"Isaiah?" She tries to sit up but falls back, weak.

"It's me, Til. You're gonna be okay."

"Henry…"

"I know. I got him. Mark too."

She nods and then her eyes widen. "Noah." She tries to scramble off of my lap, but I hold her tight.

"He's going to be fine." I twist on the floor so she can see him. "Nasty cut that Doc can stitch up. And a headache."

Tillie sags against me. "How did you know to come?"

"Blowjob."

Despite her discomfort, she laughs. Her face is bloody

and she's going to be bruised as hell but she's alive and she's still the most beautiful woman I've ever known.

"Jesus."

I glance at the doorway to see Liam standing there with his gun at his side. "Little late to the party."

"I can see that." He looks from Tillie to Noah. "Glad I brought Doc, just in case."

Doc steps around Liam and kneels next to Noah. He gets to work cleaning the large cut and when the blood is washed away, he threads his needle to start the stitches. Noah comes awake at the first poke through a flap of skin and Liam drops to his other side to hold him still.

"Doc's getting you stitched up, man. It'll be over soon."

"Where's Tillie?" Noah whispers.

"Right here," Tillie responds.

"I'm... sorry." Noah winces between words.

"Brother, you did good." I glance at Tillie and when she nods, I slide her onto the floor so I can go to Noah. "She's alive. You're alive. A little worse for the wear but it all turned out right in the end."

"I'm... I shouldn't have—"

"Stop." I snap but with no heat in the word. "I'm your president. You have to do what I say."

He starts to laugh but coughs when it causes pain. "Yes, sir."

"Let Doc finish so we can get you home."

Twenty stitches later and Doc switches his attention to Tillie. He checks her pupils and voices his concern that she could have a concussion. Then he stitches up the three cuts on her forehead. Tillie's so strong and she grits her teeth through the pain. When he's done, he packs up his bag and heads out.

"Liam, help me get them outside. Please tell me you brought the Jeep."

"Yeah, Doc drove it just in case."

Liam helps Noah up and shoulders some of his weight as he takes him out to the waiting vehicle. I bend and scoop Tillie up in my arms.

"I can walk," she protests.

"I know."

"So put me down."

"Not a fucking chance in hell."

EPILOGUE

TILLIE

A month later...

"Well, Peanut, you pulled it off again."

I smile up at my dad from my seat next to Isaiah. I look around me to take in all of the people at this year's Survivors Celebration. When my eyes land on Susie holding Curt and laughing at her older children, Carrie and Chad, as they bounce on the trampoline, my heart soars.

"I had a lot of help." I lean into Isaiah and savor the feel of him.

When the police arrived at the shelter on that fateful day, they grilled Karen about what happened. She told them the truth and it wasn't long before they showed up to the club to question me, Isaiah, and Noah. Liam and Doc were left out of it. Once all of the information, namely that Henry and Mark were stepbrothers, got out, no charges were filed against Isaiah for their deaths. Even small towns will do anything to avoid a scandal.

Isaiah has since officially moved in. The arrangement was

always meant to be temporary but neither of us wants temporary anymore. I glance at my hand and see the diamond winking at me from my ring finger. He proposed to me a week after the incident. I was worried that when the time came for that that I would have doubts or still be scared but I wasn't. Not at all. I said yes before he even got the question out.

Of course, we immediately told our families. I think, other than Isaiah and me, Isabelle was the most excited. According to her, now we'll be real sisters. Sure, it'll be legal and all, but I don't need to marry her brother to think of her as my sister. She and Lila are equally important to me.

Thoughts of Lila have me looking around again. I haven't seen her all day and she's usually the first one to play with the kids.

"Hey, Dad, where's Lila? I haven't seen her."

He glances at his cell, presumably to check the time. "I don't know. She said she was going to be late, but I thought she'd be here by now."

"Have you tried to call her?" Isaiah asks.

"No." I lift my own cell off the picnic table and press the speed dial button for Lila. The call goes straight to voicemail. "Huh."

"What?"

"Went to voicemail. She never lets her phone die. She lives and dies by that thing."

"I'm sure she's fine. I know she's got finals coming up so maybe she's still studying. If we don't hear from her in a few hours, we'll start to worry."

"Today is a day to celebrate," Isaiah reminds me. "No worrying for you."

"Right. Okay." I shake my head to rid it of my concern. It doesn't work but I can pretend. "What do you say we start wrapping this up. I'm getting ready to go home."

"Are you sure?"

"Yeah. It's been going on for six hours already. We've done the recognition ceremony, we've eaten, the kids have played and had their faces painted. Everyone is on a sugar high. I'd say all these mamas will be glad to get home and get them all in bed."

"That's a very valid point." Isaiah stands and helps me up. "Let's make the final rounds and then I'll get you home. They can all head out at their own pace then."

We do just that and it's an hour later before I say my last 'goodbye'. I climb on the back of Nyx, behind the love of my life, and rest my cheek against his back. I'm exhausted so it's a good thing that I only have to stay awake for a few minute ride.

The night air is cold, and I shiver the entire way home. Isaiah parks his bike in the garage, next to mine, and carries me inside and straight up to bed. He lays me down and begins to methodically strip my clothes off. When he reaches my scars, he traces each one with a fingertip.

"Never again, Til," he pleads.

"Never again."

"I can't stand to see you hurt, even if it is at your own hands."

I reach up and cup his cheek. "Isaiah, I promise. Never again."

"I love you, Til."

"I love you, too."

Isaiah's eyes get shiny and worry sneaks its way into my heart. "What's wrong?" I ask.

"So many years, so many hours and minutes and seconds… all without you."

"Oh, love, don't you get it?"

"Get what?"

"You were never without me." I flatten my hand against

his racing heart. "I was always right here." I then take his hand and place it against my chest. "Just like you were always right here. Always."

"Always."

BONUS CHAPTER

Need more of Tillie and Isaiah? Sign up for my newsletter at andirhodes.com for an EXCLUSIVE bonus chapter, as well as updates on upcoming novels and giveaways.

SNEAK PEEK AT BROKEN WINGS

BOOK TWO IN THE BROKEN REBEL BROTHERHOOD: NEXT GENERATION SERIES

Lila...

My father is one of the founding members of the Broken Rebel Brotherhood and my sister is with the current president. Needless to say, I'm overprotected. I've learned how to lie and keep secrets in order to have my fun but at nineteen, I had no clue what kind of trouble the real world would present.

When a monster rears its ugly head, I seek protection from the last person that should be giving it: my best friend's brother. Little do I know, they have secrets of their own. Secrets that put my life in jeopardy far worse than I ever did. But I can't seem to walk away from what I think Cooper can provide me and what I have no right asking him for: safety.

Cooper...

Living in Indiana wasn't what I'd pictured for my life. Caring for my younger sisters when we had no one else to turn to definitely wasn't on my agenda. But opening my own tattoo shop and building a life that didn't revolve around drugs, guns, and chaos has always been my dream and now it's my saving grace.

But when my sister's best friend comes into the picture, my newly established peace is thrown off balance. My world shifts and I'm tossed head first into threats and violence that I never saw coming. I want to turn her away but I can't. Every time she's near, my heart skips a beat. I know that, no matter how many times I tell myself it's a terrible idea, I will protect her life with my own. Even if it means going up against evil I thought I left behind.

PROLOGUE

LILA

"Don't forget about the Survivor's Celebration today."

I pull my cell phone away from my face and glare at the screen. Like I could forget about Tillie's big event. Like I could forget about anything related to the club or Tillie and her 'incredible accomplishments'. No one will let me forget.

I tap the speakerphone icon. "I won't Dad," I assure him, as I roll my eyes.

Cammi slaps a hand over her mouth to stifle her laugh. She's my best friend, my ride or die, my sidekick for all things trouble.

"It starts in an hour, you know," he reminds me.

"I know." I sigh dramatically. "How could I forget?"

"You better lose the attitude little girl."

"Sorry, Daddy."

Again, I roll my eyes. I've learned how to play the role he wants me to play, the role the entire club wants me to play. I'm the youngest child of the Broken Rebel Brotherhood founding members and I've felt that every single day of my life. I love my family, the club, but I want the chance to live my own life. I need to figure out who I am without the club at my back.

"We'll see you soon."

"I may be late. Cammi and I are studying for finals."

The lie slips off my tongue easier than it should. Then again, I've lied to my parents a lot lately. For example, they think I still live in the dorms on campus when in actuality, I moved out at the end of last semester so I could live with my boyfriend, Drake.

I try to ignore the pain that hits me when I think of Drake. The bitterness. He kicked me out after a few weeks, saying that he 'needed space' and I've since been staying with Cammi and her younger sister and older brother. I know that if they knew the truth, the full force of the Brotherhood would be paying him a visit and that's the last thing I need.

"Just don't be too late. You know how much this means to Tillie and with everything that she's been through lately, I'd hate to see her disappointed."

"I'll do my best," I tell him. "I promise."

You're going straight to Hell for that, Lila Rose.

I may not be bothered by lying to my parents but one thing I pride myself on is never making a promise that I can't keep. Or won't keep. But sometimes the situation warrants a break from the norm. And today is definitely one of those times.

Drake called me yesterday and invited me to a party at his place. He even said I could invite Cammi, who he never got along with. I know that there'll be drugs and that was why he needed that space in the first place but I convince myself that I can overlook that. That the drugs don't matter. Because I love him.

"Love you," Dad says before disconnecting the call.

"Holy shit, Lila," Cammi exclaims as soon as she sees that

the call has ended. "You know you're not going to make it to that Celebration."

I drop my phone on my lap. "I know. But how can I pass up this party, Cam? Drake has been weird lately and I'm hoping that the fact that he wants me there is a step in the right direction."

"Drake is an asshole." There's a bite to her tone that I'm getting used to any time Drake is brought up.

"Why did you agree to come then?" I snap back. "I can go by myself."

"Well, for one, I'm not going to let you go alone," she replies with less heat behind the words. "And two, it's a fucking party."

We both fall back onto her bed and giggle like high school girls rather than the nineteen-year olds we are. Neither one of us had what you would call a normal childhood. There was always some danger or another that the Brotherhood was fighting, which meant that I wasn't granted much freedom. As for Cammi, she and her younger sister, Carmen, were raised by their older brother Cooper. Cooper has shielded them both from as much as humanly possible.

A knock on the door startles us both and we quickly pull ourselves together.

"What?" Cammi calls out.

"Can I come in?" her brother asks.

She rolls her eyes, much like I did. "If you have to."

The door swings open and Cooper steps through. Every time I see him it's like a sucker punch to the gut. He's fucking hot as hell. And he's also six years older than me and totally off-limits.

"I thought you two were going to that celebration thing?"

His gaze swings from Cammi to me. Butterflies dance in my belly at his scrutiny, even though his stare doesn't even come close to indicating he's feeling what I'm feeling.

"Oh, we are," I assure him when Cammi remains silent. "We, um, just wanted to get some last minute studying in for finals."

Cooper folds his arms over his chest and black ink peeks out from under the sleeve of his t-shirt. I've never seen what his tattoo is but it looks like a bottom rocker of an MC tattoo. Anytime I've brought it up with Cammi, she shuts down, so I quit asking. It's intriguing though.

"Where are your books?" Cooper looks around the room. "Don't you need books to study?"

Shit!

"We just put them away," Cammi rushes to explain. "We need to change and then we'll be good to go."

Cooper sighs and scrubs a hand over his beard. He looks tired but then again, he always looks tired. I know he owns his own tattoo shop so it must be all the hours he's putting in there.

"Okay. Don't be home too late though."

"We won't."

Cammi jumps up and gives her brother a hug. It takes a minute, but he wraps his arms around her to return the gesture. As much shit as she gives her brother, Cammi loves him.

After Cooper closes the door behind him, Cammi whirls around to face me.

"Now the fun begins." A huge grin spreads across her face. "Where do you want to stop to switch outfits? Because if we leave here in anything less than a baggy hoodie and jeans, Cooper will have a fit."

"We can change at Drake's apartment." I lean down to pick up the bag I already packed for just that purpose. "That's why we're going early." I wiggle my eyebrows at her.

"Works for me."

It takes us another half hour to get out of the house

because Cooper grilled Cammi, again, about what we were doing and when we'd be back. Apparently, he was satisfied with the answers because he didn't give her as much shit as he normally would about her driving their shared Honda Civic.

It takes ten minutes to make the drive to Drake's apartment and when we pull into the parking lot, I see him standing outside on his balcony, as if watching for me. I open the passenger door and step out, waving to him when I shut the door behind me.

He waves back and smiles, but the smile slips when he sees Cammi step out on the other side. Drake quickly masks his reaction but it's too late. For a moment, I consider saying 'fuck this' and going to the Survivor Celebration that Tillie throws for the residents of her domestic violence shelter but the idea quickly disappears.

I want to have fun for real, not spend my Saturday pretending. With my new resolve in place, Cammi and I walk inside. Drake says it's okay if we use the bathroom to get ready and we do just that.

If I had known what would be waiting for me on the other side of all of my fun, I'd have gone with my gut and gotten the fuck out of Dodge.

ABOUT THE AUTHOR

Andi Rhodes is an author whose passion is creating romance from chaos in all her books! She writes MC (motorcycle club) romance with a generous helping of suspense and doesn't shy away from the more difficult topics. Her books can be triggering for some so consider yourself warned. Andi also ensures each book ends with the couple getting their HEA! Most importantly, Andi is living her real life HEA with her husband and their boxers.

For access to release info, updates, and exclusive content, be sure to sign up for Andi's newsletter at andirhodes.com.

ALSO BY ANDI RHODES

Broken Rebel Brotherhood

Broken Souls

Broken Innocence

Broken Boundaries

Broken Rebel Brotherhood: Complete Series Box set

Broken Rebel Brotherhood: Next Generation

Broken Hearts

Broken Wings

Broken Mind

Bastards and Badges

Stark Revenge

Slade's Fall

Jett's Guard

Soulless Kings MC

Fender

Joker

Piston

Greaser

Riker

Trainwreck

Squirrel

Gibson

Satan's Legacy MC

Snow's Angel

Toga's Demons

Magic's Torment

Printed in Great Britain
by Amazon

46787439R00138